nuclear HEAT

THE FIREWORK GIRLS

JORDYN WHITE

LARGE PRINT EDITION

Published by Velvet Pen Books
United States of America

www.jordynwhitebooks.com

ISBN 978-1-945261-45-9

Printed in the USA

Cover Design: Letitia Hasser | RBA Designs

Books by Jordyn White
Available in Large Print:

Firework Girls Series

Forbidden Heat
Midnight Heat
Eternal Heat
Nuclear Heat
Holiday Heat

Beautiful Rivers Series

Beautiful Mine
Beautiful Fall
Beautiful Dark
Beautiful Deep

Hearts on Fire Series

Heart of Glass

Nuclear Heat

Chapter 1

Samantha (That's Sam to You) Lawson

One more Firework Girl succumbs to marriage. I'm happy for her and everything, but it goes without saying: that will never be me.

Last weekend, Ashley and Erik got hitched in this gorgeous old stone church in Boise. Apparently, it's the first place they ever performed in the same building, and her first piano performance ever. It was for some competition clear back when they were in high school. So she puts on this (admittedly) gorgeous lace, white wedding gown and curls her long, beautiful hair with flowers and lace, and Erik puts on this tux that (let's face it) isn't that different from a suit, and we all put on our finest and trot over to Boise and watch them get married and have a big party afterward and then we all go home.

I mean, I like weddings all right, I guess. You know, they're fine. But I don't think I've ever once dreamed about what colors I'd use to decorate some reception hall or what kind of white dress I'd wear. Honestly, I'd probably burst into flames if I tried to step into a church in a white dress.

Anyway, our genuinely adorable lovebirds are getting ready to start a national tour (because they fucking rock the piano like nobody's business) and decided to tie the knot first. They'll be gone off and on all summer, before heading back to Rosebrook so Erik can finish his second year of grad school at Hartman College.

It's all good, you know. Like I said, I'm happy for them. I think they can make it work, and that's the most important thing. But even though Isabella, Chloe, and now Ashley all have their man—you know, the man—they went through a hell of a lot of heartache to get there.

I don't need to be as smart as Isabella to know I can live without all that drama. Every

2

time someone asks me if I hope to fall in love someday, I can only think, what for? What do you get out of it? Sex and companionship? I've never had any trouble fulfilling the first need, and I have my friends for the second. If you try to put sex and companionship in the same relationship, that's when you're destined to fuck things up.

Especially for a girl like me.

Well, a girl with my background anyway. Let's put it like that.

I'll give you the short version. No need to get sappy about it. My dad's an absentee, alcoholic fuck up who's spent a couple stints in jail and (probably) hard-wired me to fall in love with an asshole just like him.

That's how it works. I read all about it the same year in high school I was learning about genetic makeup and my increased likelihood of being an alcoholic myself (thanks dad). From what I understand, I could try to fight things all I want, but the truth is, girls fall in love with what they're used to. We can't help it. So, thank you, but no.

I decided a long time ago I can have sex, but I won't get attached, and I can drink, but I'll never get smashed. It's really not that complicated.

And let me tell you what, life is pretty grand. Turns out, the no-strings attached policy is a rockin' way to go. Last night I had a little naked time with a guy who's a solid 8 out of 10 in the sack and who had zero complaints about me going home afterward to sleep in my own bed.

(I have a super-plush top, king-sized mattress and a collection of the best feather-down pillows ever. That guy had two pillows. Two.)

Today, I'm with one of my best friends, Jack. Now there's companionship. No drama with this guy, that's for sure.

He showed up at my house this morning to help tear out the gawd-awful carpeting of the forty-year-old house I bought at a bargain price last year. I finally decided it's time to start refurbishing things, but neither one of us were in the mood for it today. Especially with those blue skies calling. It's fucking gorgeous out. Jack suggested we ditch the carpet and make the hour and a half drive from Rosebrook to Swan Pointe and spend our day at the Central California coast. It took me approximately three seconds to agree.

Two hours later, we're settling into our low beach chairs with my oversized bag between us, filled with the snacks we picked up on the way. My mini cooler is stocked with a few beers and several bottles of water. The vast ocean stretches out in front of us, the late morning sun glinting on the water. The waves crash along shore, then give a kind of fizzing sound as they reach high up onto land before retreating back into the water.

I love that sound. I close my eyes and sink deeper into my chair. The warm sun is already starting to heat up my skin.

"Oh yeah," I say. "This is way better than tearing out carpet."

"I still think we should knock down the wall first."

"Meh." Jack's been trying to convince me to tear out a wall and open up the space between the kitchen and dining room, but man. It sounds like such a pain. Even with him helping me. Anyway, I think he just wants to take a sledgehammer to something.

"It'll look so much better, though."

Eyes still closed, I shrug a noncommittal acknowledgment. Yeah, it'd look better, but... I take a deep, relaxing breath. The warm sun is making me too cozy to think about that weird wall in the house. There's a million weird things about that house. I can't fix all of them.

"Oh—" he says and I glance over at him. He's long and lanky, this guy. All arms and legs and that shaggy hair Ashley calls his Benedict Cumberbatch look. Only Sherlock doesn't have the striking, electric blue eyes Jack does. It's his secret weapon, I think, because he knows good and well the girls go ga-ga over those eyes.

His tan legs and bare feet are stretched out on the sand, and he's digging into the bag between us. Instead of bringing out something to eat, like I expected, he pulls out the bottle of sunscreen.

"Oh yeah." I sit up and hold out my hand. "Thanks."

He deposits a generous dollop of the white stuff onto my palm before putting some on his own. As we start working it into our arms, I breathe in that invigorating summer smell of suntan lotion.

Jack continues. "It'll be easy. The carpet's coming up in the dining room anyway, so you don't even have to worry about protecting the floor. We knock down the wall, patch up the hole, then lay down the new flooring."

"I don't know." I grab the bottle and get more lotion. Before I put it back, he holds out his hand and this time, I give some to him.

"It's only one extra step," he says as we start lathering up our legs.

"Two. Tearing it down and patching the wall."

"But then it's only ten more inches of flooring and that stupid wall is gone."

"You just want to smash the shit out of something."

He grins.

"You're such a boy," I say easily. I finish up my legs and turn my back to him. He starts applying lotion to my shoulders and back, tucking his fingers underneath the string of my bikini, to make sure he doesn't miss anything.

"Two tiny, little steps."

"Three!" I say, suddenly, thinking of something else. "We'll have to cart out all the junk. I don't even know where to take it."

"I'll handle it. Come on, Sammy. Just think how much better your table will fit."

I sigh. My table would fit better and I do hate that stupid wall. I'm starting to relent, but I'm not willing to say so yet.

He finishes my back and we both turn so I can do his. I squeeze the lotion directly onto his shoulder blades, a white line on his tan skin.

"So what's the latest on Maria?" I start to rub the lotion onto his firm back. I'm changing the subject and he knows it, but I do want an update. I haven't heard much about her lately, though, so I have a feeling I know already.

He groans.

"That good, huh?" I suppress a laugh, for his sake, but I'm grinning. Jack and his girls. I swear.

I get more lotion and rub it along his lower back and sides. He's solid muscle, this boy. If we weren't such good friends...

"I just couldn't do it," he says. "She was driving me crazy."

This time I do laugh. "Hey, at least it's a new record. You made it three whole weeks."

He groans and I laugh again.

"I don't know why you're forcing it. Who cares if it goes anywhere or not?" Jack's been obsessed with finding a 'relationship' lately. Hell, if I know why. It's like he thinks he's supposed to, but I don't think he really wants it. He'd be making completely different decisions if he did.

I finish up with the lotion and we settle back into our chairs. I drop the bottle back in the bag and he goes fishing in it again. This time he does pull out a snack. Doritos. Good choice. I want some, too.

He tears it open with one quick movement, then holds the open bag in my direction. I dig in and pull out a handful.

"Don't you sometimes think..." he begins, but then he frowns. He takes out a couple chips and chomps on them instead.

"What?" I pop a chip in my mouth. Tangy cool ranch. Mmmm.

"Well." He exhales. "I don't know, I see the kind of relationships other people have and think, I don't know. It'd be nice, you know?"

This again. "Other people like who?"

He gives me an incredulous look. "Ashley and Erik. Chloe and Grayson. Isabella and—"

"Pisssh. They don't count."

"Why not?"

"Because they weren't fuck ups to start with, so they've got a fighting chance."

"I'm not a fuck up."

"Of course not," I say and I mean it. His family's pretty amazing too, so he doesn't have all the bad programming I probably do. But some people just aren't the relationship type. Since I met him, he's been through more girls than I have guys, and that's saying something. Lately he's been trying to force this whole relationship thing, and it's been an epic disaster.

Jack's just not like that. He's like me. Free as a bird. Comfortable in his own skin. Not needing anyone else to make him complete.

It's way past time for him to just accept that about himself.

I chew on a few more chips, then say, "Jack, you keep saying you want a relationship with someone, but you obviously don't."

"What do you mean?" He digs for more chips, the bag crinkling. "Yes, I do."

He hands me the bag and I take a couple more chips. "No, you don't. If you did, you wouldn't keep picking up these bimbos." I down one chip and hold the next one at the ready while I'm munching.

"They're not bimbos." We've joked around plenty about the type of women he goes for. His job is to deny it, as if he doesn't know. I don't ever push things, because we're just messing around anyway, but come on. He needs to see what he's been doing lately and stop torturing himself.

I look at him with a serious expression. His vibrant, blue eyes meet mine and I dare him to deny it again.

He sits back, frowning at the ocean. His chips are in his open hand, waiting.

I laugh. "It's alright, sweetie. Nothing wrong with picking up good-time girls when that's all you're after."

"Is that what I'm doing?" he says quietly.

I cock my head at him. Why's he so worried about this?

"Babe, if you really wanted a relationship, you'd be going after a completely different kind of girl. Maybe you need to ask yourself why you're not."

"Huh," he says, as if this is a revelation. I grin and drop the chip bag next to my chair and start digging around for the Milano mint cookies. He's finally made short work of his chips, so I hand him a couple cookies and take a bite of one myself, gazing back at the ocean.

We don't talk for several minutes. It's just easy companionship and the sound of surf, seagulls, and some kids stomping all over their abandoned attempt at a sandcastle.

My phone goes off. It's in the string bag I use for our cash, credit cards, IDs, and keys. I dig it out, mainly so I can silence it, which I forgot to do. The last thing I want to do on the beach is be pestered by my phone. By the time I pull it out, I've missed the call. It was from my mom and I think about calling her back, but if it was important, she'd call again or text.

I silence my phone. Before I put it away, a text from her comes through. I can only see a bit of the text in the preview, but it's enough to make me freeze.

Hi honey. Thought I should let you know your dad's been—

I drop the phone to my lap and frown out at the ocean. A creeping feeling starts somewhere inside me and oozes out until it's all over my skin.

"What's up?" Jack asks.

I take a hard breath and steel myself. Whatever it is, I'm not going to let it ruin my beach day. I erect that handy wall I keep inside myself and swipe my phone so I can silently read the rest of mom's text.

Hi honey. Thought I should let you know your dad's been calling. I'm not answering. He's left some messages. He mentioned you in the last one. I don't think he has your address but you may want to keep an eye out.

That creeping feeling blooms into full-on dread. It's ballooning almost out of control as I consider all the possibilities implied by my mom's message. I haven't heard from this asshole in years, and neither has she. What the fuck does he want?

"Sam?"

I huff, and drop my phone in my bag. "My dad's been trying to contact my mom." I say it with a 'no big deal' tone in my voice, for my sake more than Jack's. He knows the story, anyway. But I'm irritated that I'm letting just the mention of my dad get under my skin.

Jack pulls out my phone and reads the text.

"What's that mean?" he asks, sounding concerned. That's not helping me.

I shrug. "Fuck if I know." Translation: I don't want to talk about it.

I'm not playing either. I really don't. I'm here for the beach and I'm going to fucking enjoy it. I just have to put this out of my mind. There's nothing I can do about it anyway.

"Hmm." Jack puts my phone back in the bag and resumes his snacking. He hands over a cookie but I shake my head. I've lost my appetite.

After a few minutes, my heart's pounding too hard and I can't seem to relax. It pisses me off, too. All these years later, and look what that asshole does to me. He's not even here.

Jack stands up suddenly, brushes the crumbs off his shorts, and extends his hand to me. "Come on, Shorty." I'm a scant five feet four inches and Jack never lets me forget it.

I glance at his hand, then squint up at him. "What?" I ask, too grouchy to try to read his mind.

Instead of answering, he grabs my hand, pulls me into an abrupt stand, bends over, and lifts me over his shoulders like a sack of potatoes. I feel the swoop in my stomach as he raises me up and starts running.

I half scream, half laugh. "Jack! No!"

Hanging upside down, I see his rear end—some grains of sand sticking to it—and his bare legs kicking up sand as he rushes us toward the water. This wouldn't be the first time Jack has sneak attacked me, so when he's thigh-deep in the waves and hefts me unceremoniously over his shoulder, I know to take a deep breath before I go under.

My body, warm from lying in the sun, jolts from the shock of the cold water. I come up gasping. "Oh, you're a dead man." I scan the water quickly until my eyes land on him. He's grinning at me and slowly backing up. He wants me to catch him, or he'd be bounding away and well out of reach. No way can I outrun those long legs.

I still feel some of the blackness my mom's text created, deep inside my chest, but Jack found the perfect thing to chase it away and I'm all in. I cup both hands and skim them sharply across the surface of the water in his direction, sending an impressive spray toward his face. Laughing, he turns away and I lunge at him, landing hard against his back and wrapping my arms around his neck.

He starts to sink down so he can go underwater, but hangs onto my forearms so I can't break free and drags me with him. The sound of an oncoming wave is deadened once I'm under the water, and we're pulled slightly toward shore as the wave goes through.

He releases me and we come up again, grinning at each other. "Brat." I spray him again.

He laughs his big Jack laugh and just like that I'm back to being me again, with no darkness pulling on me. We mess around a bit more, then take to jumping over the oncoming waves. Once we've worn ourselves out, we haul our tails onto the sand, water beading up on our skin. Jack shakes his head, water splaying everywhere and his long, wet locks hanging down in that way that makes him look so adorable.

"So, are we tearing out that wall or what?" His feet sink into deep pockets of sand as we make our way back to our chairs.

"Yeah," I say. "What the hell."

After several hours of alternating between lounging on the sand and playing in the water, along with making a respectable dent in the snack bag, we finally pack it in and start heading for his truck. He's in a good spot, in the parking lot right next to the beach; usually, we have to park on a side street somewhere and hoof it. But even though we're parked close, we still have to cross a good stretch of sand and haul ourselves and all our crap up a sandy hill. When we finally deposit everything in the back of his truck, I'm hot and ready to go.

Jack looks back to the beach, toward a cluster of food trucks farther down shore. "I'm craving some gelato."

"Dude, we just got up here."

"But it's only right down there." He turns toward me and grins.

I see he wants it, but I'm not keen on walking all the way back down. I'm about to suggest we just go through a drive-thru somewhere on our way home and get some shakes, but he says, "Come on, Shorty. I'll even give you a ride."

He gives me his puppy dog look and I roll my eyes. "Oh fine." I grab my little string bag with our valuables and throw it on my back.

He practically bounces on his heels, big kid that he is, and turns and lowers himself a bit so I can climb on. I throw my arms around his neck and he picks me up easily, hooking his arms under my knees.

Giving in to my laziness, I rest my chin on his shoulder as he carts me back down the hill.

For a moment, my mind flits back to my father. I haven't seen him in over four years. The last time, he showed up at the dorms my sophomore year, not long after my grandmother passed away. (The time before that was the horrible encounter with me and my mom, my senior year of high school.) Anyway, this time, I was in the dorm's common room. With the girls, thank God. They had never seen him but knew the story. I had a class starting soon, and when my dad said he'd walk with me, Isabella pretended to have class too so I wouldn't be alone with him. I was grateful, even though that meant she saw how I am around him. It's kind of embarrassing.

Anyway, he said he'd wait for me to get out of class, then take me to dinner. As if. I let him give me a gruff hug—hell, if I know why—and that was that. By the time I got out of class, he was gone and I haven't seen him since.

Just as well.

I don't need him anyway. I've got Jack and my girls. I'm fine.

I tilt my head, my chin still on Jack's shoulder, so I can see his profile. He's got that look he gets when he's hungry and heading for food and it makes me smile. My friends always make me feel better.

I have to admit, now that I can smell the sweet aroma of waffle cones at the gelato truck, and get a whiff of seasoned meat from the Mexican food truck, my stomach decides it's suddenly ravenous. As if I haven't already eaten half my body weight in chips and cookies.

"We should get some street tacos, too."

"Darlin'," Jack says, "you read my mind."

Chapter 2

Jack Thomas Anderson

When Emily first asked me out on a date, I almost said no. She's a new client who has the potential to give me a steady stream of web design jobs, so that's one reason. The other is, she's not the kind of girl I usually go for.

But I've been thinking about what Sam said. Why <u>do</u> I keep going for the... okay, I'm not going to call them bimbos. They're just a little...

I hear Sam's voice in my head: "Shallow. Ditsy. Princess wannabes."

More like, out to have a good time and enjoy life. Hell, I've more or less always been after the same thing. It's not like there's a problem with that.

Except...

Okay, here it is. I'm getting kind of tired of the rotating girl thing. I'd never admit that to my guy friends, because then I'd have to turn in my Man Card. But it's true. And other guys obviously get to that point eventually, too, since I see plenty of them falling in love and settling down with one woman. I'm not the only guy who wants it.

And if you want something, you should go for it, right?

Besides, it's probably time I look for a real relationship since I'm kind of, sort of a grown up now (even if I don't always feel like it). With a little nudge from Sam, I fell backwards into full-time freelancing straight out of college. I do a little bit of software design and a whole lot of web building, which I like better, and make pretty good money. Okay, great money. Business is booming, actually. I've even been invited to speak on responsive web design at a conference in Seattle at the beginning of next month.

Emily will be there too, if I remember correctly, which brings me back to her. We're at Java Hut, a coffee shop in downtown Rosebrook where I have most my client meetings, since I work from home. She's sitting across from me finishing off her peach green tea, which she orders every single time we meet. She's an attractive woman, with shoulder-length brown hair and a pretty smile. She works for a small-business consulting company, and called on me to help one of her clients get their websites set up. We just wrapped up the meeting when, out of the blue, she asked me out.

As I said, I was going to say no. But then I realize the last word Sam or anyone could use to describe her is "bimbo." She's pretty in a classy way, and smart and responsible, and doesn't seem like the one-night stand type. In fact, I'd be willing to bet on whether or not she'd sleep with a guy on the first date. (My money's on "Hell, no".)

So, next thing I know, I'm saying, "Sure, that'd be great."

Why the hell not?

After we make plans for Saturday, I don't give it much more thought though. I head home and put in another hour or so of work, primarily making notes about the project with Emily and sending out half a dozen emails to various clients and colleagues in the field.

That done, I shut down my laptop for the day and send Sam a text: <u>Need me to pick up anything?</u>

Sam: Ice. Thx.

I'm having dinner at Sam's house like I do probably on a weekly basis anyway, but tonight is special. Tonight, we're celebrating the return of our long-lost Firework Girl.

"Bella, babe!" I holler as I walk into Sam's kitchen to see Isabella and her husband, Shane, standing around the island. Isabella breaks into a grin and gives me an enthusiastic hug. Sam takes the bag of ice out of my hand just in time for me to give a proper hug back. I just saw Isabella a few weeks ago for Ashley's wedding, but this is different. Now she's back in Rosebrook where she belongs, and this time, to stay.

I try to reign things in with the Firework Girls who now have Guys, but I'm so happy she's moving back I can't resist lifting her off her feet. Being the tall, Greek beauty she is, I can only lift her a bit. "Ah, it's good to have you back, sweetheart."

"Thanks, Jack," she says, smiling at me as I set her down and release her. "I'm happy to be back." I smile and give Shane a friendly handshake. I haven't had a chance to get to know him much, since they've been living in Boston for the last two years while Isabella got her Masters in microbiology, but I like him. He's crazy about Isabella and treats her the way she deserves to be treated, so he's all right by me. Even if he <u>was</u> her philosophy professor when they first met. But that's another story.

As Sam heads for the cooler sitting against the far kitchen wall, the bag of ice hanging from one hand, I go over and take it from her.

"Thanks," she says, before returning to the counter where she's putting together a meat and cheese tray.

"How was the flight?" I ask Shane and Isabella, tearing the bag open and dumping the ice onto the bottles of beer already inside the cooler.

"Long," Shane says, "but not too bad. I'm glad we won't have to do it again any time soon."

Isabella got a killer job at Carson Laboratories here in town. As for Shane, I learn he just finalized getting his old job back at Hartman and will be picking up his doctoral work there.

"I figure at this rate, it'll take me approximately twenty years to finish my PhD," he says, grinning. "I'm on the fast track."

"I did offer to turn the job down," Isabella says. I know she feels responsible for all the delays to his education, even though he clearly doesn't mind too much.

"Like I'd want you to," he says. "It's such a great opportunity. Besides, you know I couldn't wait to get back here. I'm just glad Dean Jennings was willing to hire me again."

"Is he worried about old rumors resurfacing?" Sam asks, turning the light on in the oven and bending over to check on whatever delicious-smelling dinner she's got cooking in there. She's wearing skinny jeans and a sheer, off-the-shoulder top that shows the lacy, black bralette underneath. She always manages to look sexy without being sleazy. Her short, blonde hair goes off in different directions in this pretty, casual way. It's not hard to see why she has no trouble reeling in men on demand.

She returns to the cheese tray and I sneak over to peek in the oven myself. The smell has me hopeful.

Lasagna! Bingo!

"Well, it did come up in the interview," Shane says in answer to Sam's question, "obviously. But Dean Jennings thinks he did a good enough job keeping a cap on things before. After the initial..." Shane seems to be hunting for a delicate word.

"Scandal?" Sam prompts, providing her usual level of tact.

"Well, yeah. After it first happened"— meaning the affair he was having with his student, now his wife, our not-so-innocent-after-all Isabella—"things died down pretty quickly and he hasn't heard a word about it since. We're hoping it'll be okay."

"It helps that Shane's a fantastic professor and killing it with his doctoral work," Isabella pipes in.

"Are you basing that assessment on his work <u>inside</u> the classroom..." Sam says teasingly.

"Ha ha." Isabella sticks out her tongue.

I lightly grab Sam's side, making a direct hit on her tickle spot. She jumps and swats at my hand. "Hey, brat!"

I grin and take a piece of sliced salami from the stack before helping her add the rest to the tray.

"Where's Chloe?" I ask. She and Grayson aren't off travelling somewhere right now (you never know with those two), so they're supposed to be driving up from Swan Pointe to join in the celebration.

"I heard from her a few minutes before you arrived" Isabella says. "They're almost here."

"Too bad Ashley and Erik are gone," I say. They're done with their honeymoon, but in Philadelphia for the first stop of their tour.

By the time Sam and I finish the meat and cheese tray and put it in the center of the island, Chloe and Grayson arrive. She bounds in as usual, her auburn hair bouncing in enthusiasm, and gives Isabella and Shane hugs before making her way around to Sam and me. Mere seconds later, she clasps her hands to her chest and says, "Okay, not to steal anyone's thunder here, but..."

She and Grayson exchange excited grins.

I sense a potential delay to food consumption, so I swipe a piece of cheese off the tray. Just in time.

Chloe extends her left hand over the tray to reveal a rather impressive-looking engagement ring. Isabella and Sam gasp and lean over Chloe's outstretched hand. Shane and I give Grayson manly nods of approval, while I wonder how much he dropped on that rock.

Isabella's squealing, while Sam, who's not exactly the squealing type, says, "Damn, Grayson. That thing must have set you back a fortune."

"Nice, Sam," Chloe says, rolling her eyes but still grinning. Not to mention, she's still blocking access to the food.

"What?" Sam asks innocently, sneaking under Chloe's hand to grab a couple of cubes of summer sausage. I look at her hopefully and she tosses me one, before popping the other into her mouth and winking at me.

And that's why she's my favorite.

Isabella gives Chloe and Grayson congratulatory hugs and Sam follows suit. As I'm giving Chloe a hug and a kiss on the top of her head, I have to wonder why it's taken them this long to get to this point. It's been a year since they first got together, and given how fast things happened with them, I would've pegged them as married by now. Maybe now that they're engaged, though...

"So, have you set a date?" Isabella asks.

"Not yet," Chloe says simply. "Let's take this into the living room where it's more comfortable." She grabs the tray and starts to lead the party out. "So tell me about your new job, Bella."

Hmm. That's the kind of thing that makes me wonder what the deal is with those two. If they weren't so clearly happy together, I'd be worried.

The chatter of the group continues as they settle into Sam's living room, but I stay in the kitchen to help with the salad. As Sam and I pull out the ingredients and start assembling them into a bowl, she says, "Does it seem kind of weird to you that they're just now getting engaged?"

I nod, slicing grape tomatoes in two and tossing them on top of the spinach leaves in the bowl.

"Not that a year's a long time or anything." She shrugs. "I guess."

"I know what you mean, though."

"It's weird, right?" she says quietly, looking at me. "Something about it bugs me."

"Do you think they're having problems?"

She shakes her head firmly. "No. Look at how they are together."

It's true. They're pretty affectionate, and you can't fake the kind of glow they have when they look at each other.

"I mean, it almost makes me sick," Sam says, but she's just kidding. I think.

"Maybe they don't want to rush it, after starting so quickly?" I suggest.

Sam nods slowly, considering this. "Maybe."

"It kind of worries me, too," I admit.

Sam sighs. "Well, maybe it's nothing. They really do seem happy." She looks up at me, and leans in closer, "How much do you think he spent on that thing?"

I laugh. She's clearly not worried enough about Chloe to linger on it. I find that reassuring. God knows, Chloe deserves to be happy. "I don't know. A lot."

"I gotta say," she continues, popping the last tomato into her mouth and opening the container of Feta cheese, "I don't get why everyone wants diamonds so badly. Why diamonds?"

"You wouldn't want a diamond?"

"I wouldn't want to get married." She starts sprinkling the cheese over the salad. "But, no to the diamond. That's so predictable. Sapphires are way prettier, especially with silver. Don't you think?"

"Oh yes, dahling." I bat my hand at her. "But I'd want a ruby ring."

"Dork," she says, grinning.

"With little diamonds all around," I continue in a fake feminine voice, tracing a delicate circle on my left ring finger, "to symbolize each kid in the giant family I hope to have." I bat my eyelashes at her and she laughs.

"Your ring should be made of chocolate, to symbolize your giant sweet tooth."

"It'd never make it past the ceremony."

A month later, I'm driving Emily home from the airport, the streetlights winking at us in the dark. It's nearly eleven o'clock. We just got back from the Seattle conference, which turned out to advance things in both my professional <u>and</u> my personal life.

The owner of a large Seattle-based corporation approached me after my presentation and, during a discussion over drinks in the hotel's bar, offered me a sizeable contract to redesign and manage their collection of websites. Between that and my existing clients, I'm practically booked up for the rest of the year. When I texted Sam with the good news, she said she'd drink a glass of champagne in my honor. I asked, once more, if she's ready to reconsider a freelance career of her own yet. She sees how lucrative it's been for me, and with her graphic design skills, she could easily leave the PR firm she works for and go solo. I have several clients I could send her way. She says she doesn't want the hassle of running a business though.

Anyway, as for my personal life, things are moving along with Emily. We'd gone on a number of dates before the conference. I was right about her not being one to sleep with a guy on the first date. In fact, I didn't even try to kiss her. I waited all the way until date two. Go, me. After that, she wasn't exactly shy about things, but we didn't hook up until half way through the conference. She's not bad, either. Maybe not the best I've ever had, but she ranks right up there. She's also kind and confident and knows an impressive amount about business. She gave me a great tip about workflow management that I think will save significant time.

The biggest thing? She's not driving me bonkers.

I'd never say it to her that way, but she doesn't know what a milestone that is for me. I hate to admit Sam's been right about the kind of women I've dated, but being with someone for more than a couple weeks is a lot easier to manage with a woman like Emily.

I pull up to her condo on Lombard Street and kill the engine. I'm not planning on staying, but I'll help her with her bags. We're both exhausted from the trip and already agreed to call it a day. I don't know what the hell she packed for a four-day conference, but she has a massive suitcase in addition to her carry on. I haul them both out of the back and carry them up the walk.

"I can take one," she offers.

I shrug. "I got it."

She smiles wearily and starts fishing her keys out of her purse. "Thanks, Jack."

When we go inside, she gestures that I'm to leave the suitcases by the door. I'd be

36

happy to take them into her room for her, but if I do, I'd probably find the combination of a bed and a good-looking female in the same room too much to resist. I consider it anyway, but after taking another look at her tired expression, I decide to be a good boyfriend and stick to my word.

"Do you need anything else?"

She nods sleepily and throws her arms around my neck. I give her a hug and a kiss on the lips and, ultimately, leave her to her bed alone.

By the time I'm in my truck, I realize I haven't heard from Sam all day. She hasn't been feeling well the last couple days, so maybe she's just been sleeping a lot today. Still, we pretty much always touch base with each other.

I start the truck and head in the direction of home, but when I get to the intersection that would take me to Sam's house, I make the turn so I can go over and check on her. I'll just see if she needs anything. And make sure she's not avoiding the doctor. She hates doctors almost as much as she hates heights. One time she suffered with strep throat for so long, by the time I finally figured out what was going on and hauled her ass to the doctor he said she was lucky it hadn't turned into Rheumatic fever. That shit gets into your heart and really screws you up. I was pretty irritated about that one, because she'd been lying to me about how much pain she'd been in and about the fever she couldn't get to go down.

Stubborn ox.

When I pull in front of Sam's house, her car is parked in front of the garage and the lights are on in her bedroom. The front door is locked, but I use my key to get in. I'm quiet, in case she fell asleep with the light on. I cross the fluffy pink carpet in the darkened living room, making a mental note that we really need to get going on her renovations, and head down the hall. Her bedroom door is open and light is spilling into the hall.

A short, high-pitched sound—a sound of pain—causes my heart to clench and my pace to quicken. "Sam?"

I get a pain-filled gasp in answer and go through the door to find Sam lying on her side on her bed, clutching her stomach.

I hurry to her side, taking in her strained expression, her sweat-drenched hair, her flushed skin.

She looks at me, a desperate look of relief washing over her before she pinches her face in pain. "Jack," she breathes.

"What's wrong?" I put my hand on her bare arm. She's wearing a tank and sweatpants, and her skin is hot to the touch. "God, you're burning up." I put my hand to her damp forehead. Fuck, that's scary hot.

"My stomach," she says through gritted teeth. All huddled up like this, my normally tough Sam looks so tiny and helpless.

"Where does it hurt?" She'd texted that she thought maybe she had the flu, but this feels different to me. My entire body's on alert, because something seems desperately wrong.

"My stomach," she says again, unhelpfully.

"All over or just one place?" I gently lift one arm so I can feel her stomach, my mind racing through the possibilities. I check her right side first and, sure enough, when I give it just the slightest bit of pressure, she cries out.

Crap.

"Sorry, sweetheart."

I quickly check the other side, and after no reaction, I gather her into my arms and carry her back down the hall.

She's huddling against me, hot as an oven, but still manages to ask where we're going. When I tell her the ER, she groans and shakes her head against my chest, but doesn't protest more than that. She must really be hurting. I pick up the pace.

Once we're in the truck, my adrenaline's pumping and it's all I can do not to speed overly much and get us pulled over. I ask her questions I maybe should've asked her when we were texting this week, but she probably wouldn't have been straight with me anyway. In between her clenching and groaning, I get the full story. She's been dealing with nearly incapacitating pain for two full days. About an hour ago, she felt better for a bit, but then the pain came on even stronger. She's been throwing up and having all sorts of fun symptoms. She did originally think it was the flu—up until about a day ago.

Damn stubborn Sam.

I'm torn between being pissed she didn't get herself to a doctor and agonizing for her as she squirms in the seat over there. I have one hand on the wheel and the other on her back, trying to comfort her.

I don't say what I think's wrong, because I'm not sure she's in enough pain not to try to escape from my truck if she hears the word "surgery."

Still, there's only one way to get an appendix out and if I'm not mistaken, that's exactly what she's facing.

I park near the entrance, the parking spaces tinged red from the lettering over the wide, glass doors: EMERGENCY ROOM.

I carry her inside, trying not to jostle her too much as I hustle up to the front desk. For all the urgency I feel and for all the pain poor Sam's in, the next hour and thirty-three minutes feels agonizingly slow. First she's put in a gown and a bed, and questioned by one nurse after another about her symptoms, before a physician comes in and asks the same damn questions all over again. Do these people ever actually talk to each other? All I can do is sit here while she grips my hand, and try not to pummel everyone I see. Finally they do an ultrasound, confirm an inflamed appendix, and say the inevitable word: surgery.

Upon hearing this, Sam's eyes go wide and she grips my hand tighter, but she doesn't complain. I'm actually proud of what a trooper she's being. Watching her in this much pain is making _my_ stomach hurt. I can only imagine what she's going through.

They finally give her a couple IVs, one for fluids and one for her fever, and eventually come to wheel her away. I walk with her down the hallway as far as they'll let me go. Before they take her through a wide, automatic door with a big "Restricted" sign on it, I give her hand one last squeeze and plant a kiss on her hot, damp forehead.

She doesn't say a word, but our eyes lock and I see the fear in her eyes. My heart clenches in sympathy. "You'll be all right, sweetheart."

Her big blue eyes are soaking in my every word. "Promise?"

"I promise."

Those words are the first thing I think of when, an hour later, the physician comes into the waiting room wearing an expression that makes my blood turn to ice.

Chapter 3

Jack

The girls have a running joke that I rather enjoy. They like to tease one another and argue about which one of them is my favorite.

I've never said, of course.

I love all these girls like crazy. They're fun to tease and mess around with and give some loving to, but in a big brother way. They're fun to talk to and hang out with. I'm not sure how we got to be the way we are together. I don't know that any of us give it any thought. It's just how it is. Being a guy, I'm not blind to the fact that they're all gorgeous as fuck. I've had people ask me why I've never been with any of them, or call me a liar when I say I haven't. I don't know what to say to that. Yeah, they're beautiful, each in her own way. They're also amazing people and they occupy a special place in my heart.

But I have to admit, Sam is different.

It's never quite felt right to describe my feelings for her as "sisterly." It isn't that I don't feel protective of her, I do. But I don't feel sisterly about her either. The truth is, she's my best friend. More than the guys I hang with, even more than the other Firework Girls.

I love them all, but Sam's in her own category.

Maybe that's why, when the doctor explains that Sam's appendix got so inflamed it had been slowly leaking toxins into her body for some time and she's now "in danger," something big and deep and wild inside me starts to panic.

It's flailing around inside my chest but I'm standing stock still. I nod automatically as he grimly talks about the difficulty of detecting this kind of leak before surgery and discusses aggressive antibiotic treatments to deal with her "complications."

No, no, no, no, please God, no.

I'm strangely noticing details like the little chip in the top corner of his wire-rimmed glasses, and the wispy hair covering his receding hairline, and <u>no, no, no.</u>

When he says, "40% chance" my brain shuts down.

The wild thing inside me gets still and dark and cold and slides down my body and into the floor.

He ends by giving me that clinical sympathetic expression they probably teach in medical school. Seconds later I'm left in an empty surgery waiting room, watching his white coat disappear through the automatic door, and listening to my heart <u>thump, thump, thumping</u> in my ears.

By the time they tell us we can go in to see her, it's just after six o'clock the next morning and Isabella and Chloe are here as well. Ashley's in transit—she and Erik are flying back from Chicago today—so we're keeping her apprised of things via text. I'm staying in touch with Sam's mom the same way. She lives in Nevada and we haven't decided if she needs to come or not. She doesn't have the money for a ticket, of course, but I'll fly her out myself if it comes to that.

Please God, don't let it come to that.

The doctors are now describing Sam's condition as "critical, but stable" and are "cautiously optimistic" the antibiotics are working. I'm trying to follow the girls' lead and focus on words like "stable" and "optimistic," but the word "critical" is weighing in my chest and I can't get it to leave. The doctor hasn't given us an updated "percent chance" of recovery. I'm afraid to ask him for one.

We're told only two of us can go back to see her at a time, so Isabella and I go first. A petite nurse with shoes that squeak on the linoleum leads us down the broad, sterile hallway and into an ICU room packed with equipment and beeping monitors. The bed's in the middle and Sam's sleeping, as she's apparently been doing since her surgery. There's IVs attached to her right hand and a little oxygen tube hooked under her nose and behind her ears. She's so pale and frail-looking it almost doesn't seem like her. Except that it is her. My heart flips over and my chest starts to hurt.

"Aww, poor thing," Isabella whispers as I go around to the side of the bed. Sam's left hand is lying by her side. I take it automatically. It's tiny and warm and limp, and the sensation of holding it travels up my arm and to my chest and makes me hurt even more. I'm leaning over the bed slightly, looking at the face I know so well. I want to stroke her cheek and kiss her forehead, do something to comfort her, but we've been told to be careful not to wake her. I can only hover here, feeling lost and helpless.

"Here, honey," Isabella says quietly. She's brought over a plastic chair from the side of the room. "Sit down."

I do as I'm told, but I'm still holding Sam's hand and resting my arm on the hospital bed's side rails, looking at her face.

Come on, Sam. Fight this. You've got this.

Isabella pulls another chair up next to me. She puts her hand on Sam's forearm and leans against my shoulder. "She doesn't look too bad, all things considered."

I don't respond to this. She looks like hell. She looks like she's had the shit knocked out of her.

"She'll be okay, Jack. She's strong. The doctor said she's stable."

Critical but stable.

I nod to appease her.

We sit mostly in silence, but sometimes talking quietly about the inconsequential stuff people talk about in situations like this. Just stuff to pass the time and to avoid talking about the thing that <u>is</u> of consequence. The entire time my heart is beating soundly. Looking at Sam's face only makes it worse.

But I can't look away.

A few hours later, we're told Sam's improving. They hope to move her out of the ICU sometime tomorrow. Since there's only two, short slots for visiting hours in the ICU each day, and since we've all been up all night, the girls decide to go home, saying they'll be back for evening visiting hours. Chloe tells me I should go home too, and get some rest. I say I will.

Instead, after they leave I find the ICU nurse and persuade her to let me sit in Sam's room. It's most definitely against the rules, but I pull out all my best tricks to get what I want, because I can't bear the thought of Sam being in there alone.

Over the next several hours, I get good at sleeping while sitting in that hard plastic chair, but sleeping lightly enough that I'm still kind of keeping an eye on her. I'm careful to get out of the way every time a nurse comes in and almost get kicked out twice by people who aren't too thrilled about my presence.

But I manage to stay. Every time Sam opens her eyes, even if it's only for a moment before falling back asleep, I'm there.

By the time Sam's been moved upstairs and out of the ICU, she's waking up more frequently and I'm finally confident she'll recover. I stay anyway. I accidentally stood Emily up on our date Saturday night, but she was understanding once I explained the situation. The girls and their guys have been filtering in and out of Sam's room—Ashley's back in town—and when they say to me "Are you still here?" I pretend I've been home more than I have. I've gone home long enough to clean up and sleep for a couple of hours, but that's all.

I'm not sure why.

Even though I know Sam's out of danger and will be okay, something's still stirred up inside me. I can't relax. I can't leave her.

It's late afternoon now, two days after she was first admitted to the ER. Her color is starting to come back, and this time when she wakes up, she turns her head and focuses on me. For the first time, she seems to really see me. I take this improved awareness as a good sign.

I'm right by the bed, of course, but lean in a little more anyway, giving her a smile. "Hey, you."

"Hey." Her voice is dry.

"Want some water?" A few hours ago, the nurse brought in one of those huge plastic mugs with a handle, a straw, and markings on the side measuring off CCs. It was full of ice water at the time—the ice has since melted—and Sam was still sleeping as much as ever, so it seemed kind of pointless.

Sam weakly nods her head in answer, though, so I'm glad to have it now. After I give her a few sips, I settle back in the chair. I take her hand without thinking. She gives me a weak squeeze before relaxing her hand again. That makes the weird, pinched feeling I've had in my chest feel even more constricted.

"What happened?" she asks.

I fill her in, but downplay the whole I-was-scared-to-fucking-death-you-were-going-to-die-and-leave-me part. I downplay just how serious things got, in general. I do tell her she's been on a heavy-duty treatment of antibiotics and has a few more days to go.

"You'll be okay. The nurses say you're one tough cookie. Little do they know this was all just one big scheme to avoid ripping out that wall."

She gives me a weak grin. There's a little light in her eyes.

"Gotcha," she says, her voice still gravelly.

I squeeze her hand. "More water?"

She shakes her head no.

"Just a little?"

"Okay. Bossy."

She takes a little more this time, and the part of me that's been cataloguing every change makes another note in the "improving" column.

We talk a bit more and the nurse comes in to do her thing and I text updates to everyone. After about half an hour of this, Sam looks worn and sleepy again. Still, it's the longest she's been awake yet, and the first time she's really been present. Before I know it, I'm holding her hand and looking at her sleeping face.

When I first saw Sam in this hospital bed a couple days ago, I'd wanted to stroke her cheeks and kiss her forehead. She was so frail and sick. I wanted to comfort her. Now she's starting to get her color back along with a little bit of her orneriness—a good sign—but I still have that pinched, panicked feeling. I don't know why it won't go away.

Now, as I look at her, that feeling starts to take on a life of its own.

Something warm is blooming in my heart. Meanwhile a strange, queasy sort of feeling grips my stomach. I don't just want to pet her cheek and kiss her on the forehead. I want to pull her into my arms and cradle her head against my chest. I want to climb right into this bed and hold her against me, feeling her body against mine from head to toe. I want to kiss her on the forehead, and on her cheeks, and on her lips.

My heart is pounding. That warm feeling is flooding my chest, my arms, my face.

As I realize how badly I want to hold her and kiss her again and again, I feel the entire world flip over.

Oh, god.

Sam.

Is this for real? Is this what I think it is?

I look down at her hand in mine. I want to kiss that too, press my lips against her palm until I make her mine.

I look back at Sam's face and see her like I've never seen her before. My breath catches. My heartbeat is resonating in my body. Her presence washes over me and envelopes me.

Holy lord.

This little voice inside my brain is thinking, <u>But, but, but... we're friends. Just friends.</u>

We may have been friends for a long, long time, but these feelings I'm having are brand fucking new.

At that moment Ashley comes in, giving me a quick smile before looking at Sam. "Oh, she looks so much better." She deposits her purse on the counter, flips her long braid behind her, and comes over to sit beside me. "Don't you think?"

I'm barely breathing. Ashley's looking at Sam, but I'm looking at Ashley. Maybe my brain is just playing tricks on me. I'm tired from practically no sleep and exhausted from being so freaked out about losing my best friend.

Friend.

So I try it on Ashley. I try to see her the way a man might see her, a man who hasn't looked at her for years like a sister. But as I continue to stare at her, all I manage to do is draw her attention and make her give me a quizzical look. My heart draws a blank.

I try to imagine kissing her and can't do it. It's kind of freaking me out, actually.

"What?" she asks.

"Nothing."

My voice sounds funny. I look back to Sam and it all hits me again. <u>Bam.</u>

Oh, god.

Oh, god.

Oh, god.

Oh, god.

This can't be good.

Chapter 4

Sam

It took long enough, but I'm finally back to mostly feeling like my old self. It's been a couple weeks since the surgery and those god-awful stitches have finally dissolved, leaving three lovely, one-inch scars in various places. By lovely I mean thick, pink, and fucking ugly.

Oh, well. What are you gonna do? Two are pretty hidden and the doctor said the other one would fade eventually, so there's that at least, and it's not like it's the only scar I have. I'd be lying if I said I'd rather <u>not</u> have a scar screwing up my bikini belly, but at the same time, I don't think it's going to put a hitch in my groove.

Speaking of groove, I'm more than ready to go out and have some fun. Jack made me promise we'd finally tear out that stupid wall tomorrow, but in return he had to take me to our favorite bar on Eighth Street. Nothing like Rounders on a Friday night. His latest woman is out of town on business or something, so I knew he'd be free.

Things have been a little... I don't know... <u>different</u> with Jack lately. I can't put my finger on it. It's so subtle and so infrequent, it took me a while to even realize it was there.

There's no hint of that tonight, though. Talking and goofing around like we always do, we walk up to the entrance of the bar and flash our IDs. It seems kinda pointless, since the guy at the door knows us well enough by now. But Frank would get in trouble with his boss if he was caught letting us in without going through the motions.

"Hey Jack. Hey Sam." He nods us in and we weave through the crowded bar toward our favorite spot. The place is hopping and the music is pounding and it feels so good to do something <u>fun </u>and <u>normal</u> after the pain-in-the-ass hassle of the last few weeks. Between trying to recover physically, it took me a while to get caught up at work too. My co-workers did what they could for me in my absence, but when we have clients specifically requesting me to design their logos and image branding, there's just no spreading that workload around. Everyone's been patient and understanding about adjusted deadlines, but man. I'm beat from the whole thing.

We sit at a little round table and wave at Nick, the bartender, to indicate we want the usual start: a brown ale for Jack and an amber for me.

"You sure you're up for that?" Jack says.

"I'm fine." I'm jamming a little in my seat to the music and looking longingly at the dance floor. "You're gonna dance with me tonight, right?"

"I guess," he says, with an exaggerated sigh. "If I have to."

I smile.

"But only the slow songs."

"Slow songs? What the hell?"

First of all, we don't slow dance. Probably because we have an unspoken understanding that slow songs are saved for any hotties we

59

might be checking out in the bar. Not that he's in a position to check out hotties, being all "exclusive" with that Emily girl. I mentally roll my eyes. I definitely don't get that, but whatever. I haven't even met her so she can't be <u>that</u> big a deal.

Second, fast songs are my favorite and <u>no one</u> is as fun to dance with as Jack.

"You probably shouldn't be bouncing around like that."

I roll my eyes. He's doing the Mother Hen thing again. "You mean like this?" I start bouncing to the raucous music more enthusiastically.

He gives me a wry look.

I raise my arms and do my best head banging interpretation for a few seconds. I'm rewarded with his big Jack laugh, so I settle back in my seat, satisfied.

One of the waitresses brings us our drinks.

"See? I feel fine," I say, grabbing mine.

"Okay, okay."

"Anyway, explain to me why you're okay with me knocking out a wall tomorrow but not dancing tonight."

"Because I'll be the only one swinging that sledgehammer, darlin'."

Well, yeah. I can lift most things now, but I still get a bad twinge around the area of the incision if I lift really heavy things, so the sledgehammer's probably out. It's crazy how long it can take to recover from abdominal surgery. But even if I didn't have that shit going on, I doubt I'd be the one with the sledgehammer anyway. "I'll be hauling scrap out to the truck though."

He shakes his head firmly. "Nope."

Now it's my turn to give him a wry look. "Really. What the fuck am I going to be doing tomorrow?"

"Just keep me stocked on cookies and I'll be happy."

"Shall I wear heels and pearls, too?" I ask innocently.

He grins and takes a few swallows of his beer.

A group of guys approach the bar and line up, chatting easily with each other. I know one of them. By "know" I mean I know exactly the sound he makes when he's getting his happy ending. He spots me as well and gives me a sexy grin.

I straighten slightly and feel myself getting warm. It's been way too long for lots of things, turns out. I have rules about how often and how frequently I'll sleep with the same guy—no need for anyone to risk getting too attached—and the guy at the bar is well within my criteria. But, it'll have to wait for some other time. I'm here with Jack and can't just leave him. If he had a hottie he could go check out himself, that'd be fine. Or if we were here with the girls, that'd be fine too. But I'm obviously not going to leave him alone. Besides, it's nice being here with him tonight. I've missed it.

I look at him and realize he's been watching me. He's giving me a weird look.

"What?" I ask.

There's a pause that's just a half second too long before he glances at the guy at the bar, then looks away toward the dance floor. "Nothing."

See? Like this. What the hell is this?

He takes a hard swig of his beer, then pops the bottle on the table with a thud.

Okay, this is reaching a whole new level. He's been kind of off the last few weeks, but now he actually seems pissed or something.

"What's wrong with you?"

"Nothing."

I give a snort. What an awful liar. "Oh, please, Jack. You can't hide anything from me. Fess up, already."

He looks straight at me then, a serious expression on his face. Something about it tugs at me.

The smile slides off my face as I really take him in. What's this about?

"Sam…" There's something in his tone. I don't know what it is. "When you say you don't ever want a relationship, are you being serious or are you just saying that?"

What?

As if he doesn't know. I would say something smart ass, but he's definitely not kidding. He needs a straight answer, for some reason. Hell, if I know why. I have a tingling sensation down my neck, but I ignore it. "Jack, girls marry guys like their father. We can't help ourselves. And fuck if

I'm going to do that." I've said all this to him before.

"But, not all girls do."

I shrug. "Yeah, some girls escape that fate. But you don't usually know if you're one of them until it's too late. Why take the chance?"

He frowns at the bottle in his hand. "What if you met someone who's nothing like your father?"

I raise my eyebrows and he looks at me out of the corner of his eyes.

"Am I anything like your father?"

The tingling sensation down my neck travels to my shoulders and arms. "What's it got to do with you?" I feel a little uneasy. Really, really weird, actually. I'm not sure why. What's he getting at? Whatever it is, I'm cutting him off at the pass. "No," I say, firmly. "I am serious and I'm not just saying it. I will <u>never</u> be my mother."

He's frowning. Really frowning.

"Geez, Jack, what's been bothering you? Is this about that Emily chick?" Maybe she's been around too long for his pleasure. Maybe he's finally realizing that trying to force a long-term relationship isn't such a good idea after all.

"No. I mean, yes." He shakes his head in frustration. "Maybe. Kind of."

I laugh. "Well that clears things up."

He sighs.

Man, he's so tense. Maybe if I help him relax, he'll spit out whatever's on his mind. I scoot my seat behind him and get on my knees so I can reach his shoulders better. I start to massage him, close to the base of his neck. Instead of relaxing, he tenses up immediately.

A new song comes on, "Low" by Flo Rida, one of our favorites to dance to.

He gets up suddenly and turns toward me with an easy grin, extending his hand toward me. Just like that, the old Jack is back. I'm starting to get whiplash from this shit.

"Come on." He jerks his head toward the dance floor. "Let's dance."

Chapter 5

Jack

I am so, so, so fucked. And not in a good way.

I cannot get these feelings for Sam to go away. It's frustrating as hell. I can't even talk to her about it, because the last thing I want to do is screw up our friendship by making her feel weird.

Instead, I have to take her dancing and pretend I'm not completely turned on by the way she shakes that delicious body of hers.

Was I fucking blind before?

It's taking an epic amount of willpower not to have an erection every second I'm around her.

She doesn't even have to be dancing. The other day I stopped by her place when she was crashed out on the couch, on her stomach, arms and legs flailed out all over the place like they usually are when she sleeps. All I wanted to do was mount that adorable little ass and ride her until she cried out in ecstasy.

I'm starting to feel a little possessed.

The longer this goes on, the more I want to give into it. But Sam has made it clear, she really doesn't want a relationship. Not at all. Not ever.

It's torture.

Not that it matters because even if she were open to the idea of relationships in general, there's no sign she'd reciprocate feelings for me, even if I did come clean. I'm her friend. Only that. And she's supposed to be able to trust me. I'm not supposed to be fantasizing about her every time I bang my girlfriend.

Which is a whole other problem. It's kind of fucked up. I know this. But the thing is, Emily's a sweet girl. She's been open about the fact that she's developing feelings for me. I enjoy her company well enough. If it weren't for the fact that I'm, you know, burning a fucking torch for my best friend, my relationship with Emily would be fine.

You know, fine.

Sam's a closed door. Why mess things up with Emily just so I can have even _more_ time to stare longingly at a closed door?

No, if anything, Emily's my ticket to sanity. I just need to give myself time to get closer to her so I don't have to be in love with Sam anymore.

It's a sensible plan.

Sam and I simply need to go back to just being friends, like we've been for years.

Scratch that. I'm the one who needs to go back to just being friends. Sam's still there. Will always be there. The fact that that makes me want to tear down her wall with my bare hands is not her fault.

I need to get it together. I cannot risk losing this friendship. I need her.

Although...

There are those moments when I wonder if maybe she wouldn't mind more with me. I mean, I think I could make her happy. It's not so crazy, is it?

I was fishing last night at Rounders. I couldn't help it. Sometimes my fantasies about being with her get the better of me. But I wish I hadn't asked about relationships. Her answer was fucking depressing.

Yet, here I am again, sledgehammer in hand, half a wall in bits all over the floor, and all I can think about is Sam over there in her short shorts and tank top. Doesn't she <u>know</u> how good she looks? Is she <u>trying</u> to torment me?

I take aim, pull the sledgehammer back, and crash it into the wall with every bit of strength and every drop of sexual frustration I have.

It barely helps.

I can't stop wishing for her.

I'm starting to consider drastic measures.

That night we're celebrating the successful removal of a wall with Chinese takeout and a movie. We're watching <u>The Illusionist</u>, one of Sam's favorites. I like it too, but I mostly agreed to it this night because I remembered it has a great love scene that I'm hoping I can use to my advantage.

If I have the balls to pull it off.

My heart's pounding a mile a minute. I can't believe Sam can't hear it, leaning on my chest the way she is.

We're in the standard movie-watching position. This is how it works, and it's the same with all the Firework Girls. I pick any spot on the couch I want, the middle or the corner, depending on my mood. I stretch my legs on the coffee table and my arms on the back of the couch and settle in. <u>Ahhh.</u> Comfort.

Then those girls can lay all over me however they want. Usually they just lean against my chest. I don't put my arms around them, because then that's kind of like snuggling. I don't know. It's just a line we don't cross.

None of this has ever been spoken about or written down in some "Jack's Harem Rule Book."

But I think we all understand it well enough.

So, yeah. Sam's in her teeny shorts and her tank and her fucking amazing breasts are pressed right against my side. Her head's on my chest and she smells all delicious. My arms are right where they're supposed to be, on the back of the couch, and my dick should get a fucking gold medal for the endurance it's taking not to be as stiff as a board right now.

About a minute before the love scene I know is coming, I pull my hands up as if to rest them behind my head. Another acceptable position. But while my left hand goes behind my head, I casually rest my right hand on her shoulder, my forearm settling against her bare upper arm.

Yes, I realize this is kind of like the junior high yawn-and-stretch move, but she's not glaring at me or protesting yet, so fuck off.

The love scene begins at last and this is my chance. Because as much as Sam likes to be a hard-ass, I've seen her get all mushy over love scenes just like the rest of the girls, even if she tries to hide it.

And it's a hell of a scene, too. Tasteful and understated, with just the right amount of eroticism.

My hand's still on Sam's shoulder. She's perfectly still. So am I. Except my index finger slowly reaches out and touches the soft skin on the back of her neck. Eyes locked on the screen, I'm barely breathing. I gently trace my fingertip up, up, so slowly, until I reach the silky base of her hair.

She lifts her head off my chest, just slightly. I allow another fingertip to touch her neck, then another, until I'm slowly caressing her in a way I'll call "absentminded" later if I have to. But there's nothing absentminded about this. Every touch of her skin sends jolts of electricity through my arms and straight to my heart.

She slowly turns her head toward me. I leave my hand in place so I'm almost—but not quite—cradling the back of her head in my hand and almost—but not quite— holding her in my arm. I'm terrified, but I keep my eyes on her face, watching for her reaction.

She looks at me. Somber. Wondering. I don't move. I could so easily kiss those amazing lips of hers. God knows I want to. But this is as far over the line as I can go and still save face if she doesn't want it, if she really does only see me as a friend.

Our eyes lock together. Time seems to stop. Yet again, her presence washes over me and damn near consumes me. My heart is pounding and my cock is fighting a losing battle now. My god, how I want this woman.

She blinks twice, her brow twitching down slightly in confusion. A half-smile appears, like she's expecting a joke or a punchline. Then our eyes lock hard and her expression grows serious. Time stops again and I almost do it. I almost throw all caution out the window and press my lips against hers. I need to taste her. I need her. But I don't move.

And neither does she.

Until she does... away from me.

She gives a strange, short laugh and slaps my stomach lightly before angling away so she's curled up against the arm of the couch.

I feel as if the wind's been knocked out of me and I almost shiver with the chill that's dropped through my heart.

"You big dork," she says grinning.

I force a smile, too. I think, under normal circumstances, I would probably tickle her side or a foot or something.

I don't do that.

Under normal circumstances, she'd eventually uncurl and stretch out and rest her feet in my lap.

She doesn't do that either.

What we do is watch the rest of the movie without touching at all. When it's over, we exchange a couple of lame jokes and congratulate ourselves on showing that wall who was boss. Then we say goodbye and I leave her house with my answer.

She doesn't want me.

Chapter 6

Sam

I'm sitting in my living room wondering when Jack's going to show up, and trying to figure out what's up with me today. I'm feeling strangely unsettled.

Maybe it's because my body's still not at a hundred percent after the whole surgery and life-threatening infection thing.

Maybe it's because I've spent the last week staring at an empty space in my house where a wall used to be. There's still a big gash in the adjoining wall and ceiling that now needs some drywall. It's just rockwall, or whatever the hell they call it. Sheetrock?

Anyway. Maybe I've been feeling unsettled because I finally got back on the horse and picked up a guy down at Rounders last night, but it wasn't as great as it usually is. It's not that the sex was bad, exactly. It should have been great, all things considered. I've ridden that stallion before. Plus, it had been way too long, so my body was more than ready. I've been a little high-strung in that department, so he got me there just fine.

But afterwards I felt kind of... unsatisfied.

It's weird.

I mean, I get that people looking for love don't handle casual sex very well and can feel like shit afterwards. I get it. I'm not an idiot. But there are those of us who handle casual sex just fine. Since I'm one of them, the whole thing was a little perplexing.

It almost makes me wonder if... well. There was that moment with Jack last week. Somehow he was... holding me kind of, and the back of my neck had goosebumps where his fingers were touching me. I had goosebumps all over, I think. He had a strange look on his face. I have no idea what that look meant and don't really want to analyze it, to be honest. I still remember how he smelled, though. Like Jack, but more. Probably because he'd been sweating from tearing down that wall. Probably it was just that. I mean, guy sweat smells sexy. That's no shocker.

I exhale sharply and get off the couch. I'm being an idiot. That has nothing to do with anything. That moment with Jack was just... a thing. Nothing.

But feeling like I did last night after what should have been a pick up for the books, well... that's not nothing. It's not like me at all.

I head into the kitchen, looking for something to snack on. I open the pantry, but just kind of stare at everything. I really need to go shopping. I'm totally out of the good snacks. The only thing in here that's passable is fucking graham crackers.

I consider talking to Jack about this weird unsettled feeling I have. He's supposedly coming over sometime today to fix the drywall, so maybe I can talk to him about it then? When he's not being a big dork, he can give me pretty good advice. If he ever shows up. It's kind of late in the afternoon to start a project like this. Maybe we'll just blow the whole thing off today.

My phone vibrates in my pocket and I hear Jack's ringtone. Speak of the devil. "Hey. Are you on your way?" I shut the pantry and start heading for the living room.

"Not exactly." His voice has a strange quality to it. Echoey, but something else.

"You sound like you're going through a tunnel. Where are you?"

"On a plane headed to Spain."

O-kaay.

"Ha ha." I'm still trying to figure out what I hear in his voice.

"No, seriously. We land in about three hours."

I stop and the gears in my brain start working overtime. This can't be right. He's supposed to be on his way over here. "We?"

"Emily and I. It was kind of an impromptu thing, you know." His voice definitely does not sound normal. "We wanted to go and so we're going."

"To Spain?" No, he has to be joking. Surely. He's such a dork sometimes. "Look if you can't do it today, it's not a big deal. Just say so."

I hear giggling in the background. "Just a minute, honey," he says. To her, Emily. Not me. Then he laughs. Still not to me, to her. Now I can identify what I've been hearing in his voice: excitement. He's practically giddy.

What in the hell?

"You're seriously on your way to Spain. Just like that?"

"Sometimes you just have to take a leap, right?" What the fuck is that supposed to mean?

Now, thanks to Jack, my aforementioned unsettled feeling has morphed into a vague sense of dread. Probably because he's acting like an idiot and is, as a bonus, up in the air in one of those death traps they call an airplane instead of safe on the ground where he belongs. And what's he doing flying off to fucking Spain? Who does that?

I'm hovering in the middle of the living room, but I find I need to sit. Foregoing the couch, I sink to the edge of the coffee table. "When do you get back?"

There's a pause where there should have been an answer. The wheels in my head are working again.

"Jack?"

"Um. I'm not sure. It'll be awhile."

What? What the hell? I try to wrap my head around what he's saying. There's more giggling in the background. He gives her a soft laugh. It's a deep throaty laugh that makes me frown. I don't know why. "Sorry, Sam, I have to go. But I sent over a guy. His name's Ron and he owes me a favor. He'll take care of your drywall for you. Won't cost you a thing."

"But—"

"Bye, Sam."

The phone goes silent.

I bring it around and stare at it. Jack's name is still on the caller ID but the call's been disconnected. "What the fuck?"

The doorbell rings. I drop the phone to my lap and stare at the front door. I don't move.

"What. The actual. Fuck."

The doorbell rings again and I hop up, irritated that whoever's on the other side can't seem to wait one goddamned minute while a person walks to the door. I open it to find the Anti-Jack standing on my stoop: he's short, balding, and looks to be in his fifties, at least.

He gives me a broad smile. "I'm Ron. Jack sent me."

Jack sent me. That rat bastard.

"Yeah, he just called." I open the door to let him in. "It's over here."

Still frowning, I lead the Anti-Jack into the dining room. I'm still not entirely sure what's happened. How could Jack be on his way to Spain? And how can he not know when he'll be back?

I send him a quick text: <u>Let me know when you land.</u>

God, I hate airplanes.

I show Ron where the wall used to be and try to remember to act polite as he assures me he'll have me fixed up "in a jiffy."

I don't even have the energy to mentally mock the "jiffy" comment. I'm still wondering what on earth Jack is doing.

What about work? I text him.

I instantly realize Spain has Wi-Fi as well as we do, but still. Is he working from Spain now? Doesn't he need... I don't know... plug adapters or something there?

An hour later, my dining room is sporting fresh drywall, Ron is out my door in a fucking jiffy, and I've sent another half dozen texts to Jack asking him where he's staying and if she has family in Spain and doesn't she have work too and what does she do for work?

But he doesn't answer any of them.

When I go to bed, I break my self-imposed rule about no phones in the bedroom while I'm trying to sleep (I have no such rules about phones in the bedroom when I'm trying to fuck). I bring in my charger so I can keep my phone on the nightstand, within easy reach.

Around midnight I still haven't heard from him but I'm relatively sure his plane landed okay because there are no reports on the internet about a plane crash or a terrorist attack or a fucking meteor hitting an airplane or anything.

The thought crosses my mind that he may have gotten into an accident on the way from the airport to the hotel, but I'm pretty sure he's just ignoring me.

"Fine," I say out loud, turning off the light and punching down my pillow. "Whatever, Jack. Enjoy your little European fling. Whatever."

I don't sleep much that night.

Probably because I had my phone in my bedroom. I wake the next morning resolved not to charge it in there again.

Chapter 7

Jack

Part of me knows this was an act of desperation. But it's only the teeniest part of me and I'm ignoring it.

Mainly, I'm on cloud fucking nine after having such a brilliant brainstorm. One minute, I'm sitting on Emily's couch feeling miserable enough to actually say aloud: "I just fucking need to get away."

She'd sensed my mood, though she had no idea what was behind it, and started joking around about all the places we could run away to: Nantucket! Neverland! Nigeria!

See? She's not the only one who knows how to joke around with me. It's not just Sam. Emily gets me, too.

The next thing I know, we're looking at Groupon deals and I'm starting to get serious about things.

I could get away. I really could. Plus, Emily's company is pretty forward-minded, so when she's not off on a business trip, she works almost exclusively off-site in her home office.

Where I fucked her lights out after booking our flights to Spain. See? It doesn't have to be Sam.

It doesn't.

No. All I need is some distance and some time to spend with Emily without having Sam right in front of me all the time. I mean, she's still my friend. We'll always be friends. But that's clearly all she wants and so, well, fuck it. I'm just going to focus on the girl I have.

And she's great.

Really.

And Spain's fucking great. Amazing.

And when I wake up to find Emily in the bed next to me, I can almost manage not to wish it was Sam instead.

Almost.

Chapter 8

Sam

Portland, Two Years Ago

"Even in Portland, you're still Jack's girl."

That's what Ashley said several months after we all graduated from Hartman College and kind of went our separate directions. She was talking about the fact that even though Jack's still in Rosebrook and I'm up here in Portland, we talk and text so much it's practically like I'm still living there. I still chat with my girls too, so I don't know what Ashley's fussing about. Okay, the girls and I don't talk every day like Jack and I do, but it's Jack. It's always been like that. We can't use the phone just because I'm in Portland?

Speaking of Portland, I'm way fucking over it. The job I got was pretty awesome for a new college grad, but my asshole boss is driving me crazy and I seriously miss the blue skies of central California. I can't get over how often it rains here. Portland's a hip town and I'd probably fall in love with it if it weren't for all the fucking rain.

That makes Jack happy, let me tell you. He's been on me to get a job in Rosebrook ever since he found out about the job I got in Portland. He wants Isabella to move back to Rosebrook, too. And Chloe. He was not happy when she left her post-college job in Swan Pointe and moved all the way to Boise. I've no idea what the hell's in Boise, but whatever. The point is, Jack thinks the Firework Girls should all live in Rosebrook forever even though things don't usually work out that way.

Yet, for the past several months I've been hounding the Rosebrook job boards, too, like Jack's been doing for me ever since I moved here. But Rosebrook's a smaller town than Portland so there's not as much opportunity in my field. The few high-quality firms there are tiny and entrenched with long-term employees. They're just not in the market for anyone new.

At least, I didn't think they were.

Jack texts me early one morning to tell me The Adelman Group is hiring. Fucking Adelman. If I could hand-pick any company in Rosebrook to work for, it'd be them. When I do my own search for their job listing, though, I come up dry. I'm at work, so I have to be sneaky about it. I'm sneaky about my text back to Jack, too: <u>Are you sure? I don't see anything.</u>

Jack: Just wrapped up a job for their PR director and he said they need a graphic designer. I recommended you.

Me: Seriously?

Jack: Just emailed you the details. I need my drinking buddy back in town, so don't screw it up.

Me: Suck it.

I open Jack's email and start drafting a cover letter to The Adelman Group. Halfway through, my hopes are rising in my chest. I could be back in Rosebrook, close to Jack and Ashley, who's still at Hartman College working on her masters in music. And Adelman is such a good company.

I send Jack another text: <u>Thanks.</u>

He sends back a GIF of a couple drunk guys doing a fist bump, and missing. "Dork," I say, grinning.

Three weeks later I have the job, I've put in my notice, and Jack's made an impromptu drive up to Portland to help me pack.

We're sitting on the floor of my closet, half packing, half sorting crap. I have way too much crap. I have enough clothes and shoes and accessories to outfit a small country. I should've cleared things out before I moved up here, but I wasn't in the mood to deal with it, so I threw everything into boxes and hauled it up here instead. I mentioned this in passing to Jack and now here we are, a box for packing in front of me and a big trash bag for donations next to Jack.

The bag is nearly empty, even though we're nearly done with the tops. The sorting isn't going too well.

But I <u>am</u> hearing a rather entertaining story about Jack's latest girl. Or, ex-girl. Well, the problem, really, was that <u>she</u> thought she was his girl, when he thought she was just <u>a</u> girl.

Poor guy's been down this road before. The fact that he's a big softie at heart only makes it worse.

"I don't mean to make it happen." He finishes folding a shirt I've indicated is a keeper and puts it in the box. The nearly-full box. "I'll be going along with someone and think we're just having fun and next thing I know they're telling me they love me."

He has this startled look on his face and I have to laugh. I add a whole stack of shirts to the box.

"<u>Love</u> me." He shakes his head. "So then I have to go and end it and there's tears and sniffling and why does this keep happening?"

"Because you're just so <u>lovable</u>." I swat him on the chest and bat my eyelashes.

"Ugh." He holds up the last shirt in his pile and gives me a questioning look.

I forgot I even had this shirt and for good reason. When did <u>that</u> thing ever look good? I make a face and Jack tosses it into the donation bag.

Okay, there's a little progress.

"I'm starting to think you've got the right idea about repeats." He means my policy of limited encounters with the same person. But I know him too well. He's so friendly and easy-going, it's just not in his nature to keep a girl at a distance when he thinks everyone's having a good time.

I continue to "sort" the clothes in front of me and Jack starts absentmindedly poking through the shelf in front of him. There's all kinds of random crap on that shelf, so who knows what he'll find. "Oh <u>yeah</u> baby. What have we here?"

I glance at what he found. Oh, right. I forgot I had a bag of mini Snickers bars left over from the after-Easter sales. I bought two bags, because, come on, how often are <u>Snickers</u> in the post-Easter bargain bin? Since Jack hasn't been around to pilfer my food, I still have some left even though it's nearly two months later.

He slowly reaches inside the bag, looking at me questioningly, as if to say, <u>Is this up for grabs?</u> Man, we <u>have</u> been apart too long if he thinks he needs to ask. I smile and roll my eyes. He dives in, extracts a piece, tears off the wrapper, and tosses it into his mouth whole. "Mmmm," he says, his eyes rolling back.

"No food orgasms in my closet."

"What else do you have in here?" He grins and glances around before taking a handful out of the bag.

"It's a wonder you're not six hundred pounds by now."

I toss the last shirt in the box and grab a pile of scarves. Jack's very busy unwrapping and devouring his candy. "Keep. Keep. Keep." I toss one scarf after another into the box. "Donate!" I pick up a floral scarf that was outdated two seasons ago and toss it in his lap. More progress!

"This?" He picks it up. "You sure?"

"Donate," I say, tossing two more into the box.

He wraps it around his neck and gives me a serious expression. "Is this my color?"

I roll my eyes and he grins at me.

I get to the green scarf I've always loved, but that no longer goes with anything I wear on a regular basis. "Hmm."

"Keep," Jack says, tossing it into the box for me.

"How do you know?"

"If you have to hesitate, you shouldn't get rid of it."

"Shows what you know. If you have to hesitate, you shouldn't keep it. Girls only wear what they love." But I keep it in the box. "You're supposed to be helping me, you know."

"I am helping you."

I take a second to think about the progress we're making, or the lack of it. "Pull down what's on that shelf," I say, pointing. "You can just pack it. I think it's all coming with me."

He gets up obediently and starts poking around. "No more candy stashes?"

I finish with the scarves. I've only added three to the donate pile, including the one still around Jack's neck. There's something like thirty of them in the box. I sigh. Oh well. I tape it up while Jack retrieves an empty box and starts packing what's on the shelf. I push the sealed box out of the closet and start putting the contents of another shelf into Jack's box. I've given up on clearing things out. It'll take me two years to pack at the rate we're going.

"Hey," Jack says. "Cool."

He pulls down the wooden box he found and I smile. This box is probably the most precious thing I own. It's made of walnut, but about the size of a small microwave so it's not too heavy. There's a raised, embossed dragonfly on the lid.

Jack gives me a devious grin. "Are all your deep, dark secrets hidden in here? What happens if I open it?"

He settles back on the floor and I join him, the wooden box in front of us. "Open it if you dare," I say, scooting it closer to me. "It used to belong to Pandora."

"I knew there was a reason I like you."

"It was my grandmother's."

"Ah," he says softer, as I run my hands over the embossed dragonfly on the lid. "The famous grandmother."

The body of the dragonfly has started to fleck around the edges, but the outstretched wings are still iridescent blues, purples, and greens, made of cracked glass. I run my fingers over the ridged surface of each wing, just like I did when I was a little girl and the box still belonged to my grandmother.

"Have I ever showed you a picture of her?"

He shakes his head and I open the lid. The pleasant smell of old wood greets me like a familiar friend. The lavender satchel in here lost its scent long ago, though. Inside the box is a small stack of photos, a few pieces of her jewelry including the dragonfly broach, her big, broad-rimmed purple hat with the red feather, and the seashell I added to the box after she died.

My first sketchbook, which she gave me, is in here too, underneath everything else. I don't flip through it much anymore. Even though I have an eye for design that really took off once I went digital, it's painfully obvious how rough my drawing skills were back then. I keep it in spite of this because even though it's my book, it's as much about my grandma as everything else in the box. She somehow knew what drawing could become for me: a healthy way out.

I turn to the stack of photos and pick up the one on top. It's of my mother, my grandmother, and me when I was about thirteen. We're standing in front of the rose bushes in Grandma's backyard. My mother is in tight jeans and a snug, low-cut top. Her boobs look ready to bust out of prison any second. Those were her big hair days. So, yeah, she definitely fits the mold.

My grandmother is in the middle. Short. Heavy-set. Smiling. She has an arm around each one of us.

I'm the scrawny, pre-pubescent girl next to her. My hair was long back then, past my shoulders. It's not a great picture of me, but it's one of my favorites of my grandmother. It was taken after we moved in with her, not long after my mom's second divorce. My dad was still in prison then.

I hand the photo to Jack. He takes it and smiles. "Look how cute you are."

"Cut it out."

"Seriously. That's adorable." He's holding it up, his elbow resting on his knee, and looking between me and the picture.

I roll my eyes.

He winks at me and goes back to examining the photo. "This is nothing how I pictured your grandmother. She looks way too normal."

I laugh. "What's that mean?"

"You know, the way you describe her she seems larger than life."

I smile, pleased that Jack has the proper picture of her. She <u>was </u>larger than life.

"I imagined her kinda... funky and hip." He lowers the photo and notices what else is in the box. "Like that hat! I can totally see her wearing that."

I grab the stack of photos still in the box and hand it to him. "There's a picture of her in there with her hat ladies."

As he starts flipping through the photos, I pick up the dragonfly broach. It's made of colored glass and brass and is a huge gaudy thing. I'd wear it if it didn't practically scream "grandmother's jewelry." But I pull it out and look at it often enough. The dragonfly on the lid and the broach are kind of my symbols for my grandmother. And myself. Thanks to her.

Holding it in both hands, I run my thumbs over the wings. Unlike the wings on the lid of the box, these are smooth and feel substantial in my hands.

"When I was about fourteen," I say, impulsively beginning a story I've never once shared with another soul—not even my Firework Girls even though they've all seen the box and know about my grandmother—"I was in trouble with my mom again. This time for sneaking out of the house in the middle of the night."

I'm still running my thumbs over the dragonfly's wings. Out of the corner of my eye, I see Jack pause his picture-flipping to watch me.

"I was in the den by myself, pouting. I thought I was pouting because of being grounded for two months, or whatever the fuck she'd said. But it was really everything, you know? Everything that was going on back then."

I glance at him and he nods. He knows.

"So my grandmother comes in and I kind of scowl at her too, because I was just being a brat and mad and, you know..."

"Being you." He gives me a wink.

I make a face at him, but smile. "Yeah. But, you know, the hurt and angry, teenaged version. So she comes in and starts talking to me about this pin she's wearing." I lift it by the dragonfly's body and turn it in my fingers. "At first, I thought she was being really random, you know. Like, why did I care about her stupid pin?"

I lower it to my lap again, still not sure why I'm telling Jack this story, but it feels nice to tell him.

"But grandma, you know. She had this way. If she wanted me to listen to something, she could do it. It was the tone of her voice, I think. I could tell if she had something important to say and I'd start listening. On the inside, you know?"

I shrug. I can't really explain my grandmother.

"Anyway, so she tells me this cool story about the myth of the dragonfly. They used to be dragons, thousands of years ago. They represent change, growth, and power."

The weight of this particular memory settles on me. It was long ago, but it was one of those things that's stuck with me. I clearly remember my grandmother telling me the story, just like this. I look Jack in the eye, just like she looked at me all those years ago. He's still and quiet and listening, just as I had been.

"But the change they represent isn't the kind of change you see on the outside, even though they did change a lot. And the power they represent isn't the kind of physical power they had when they were dragons. They represent change of self,"—I remember my grandmother touching my heart right then—"and power of mind." I can still feel her tapping my temple lightly, winking at me.

Things no one can take from you, she'd said.

"Do you know these little guys can fly in any direction?" I say. "Up, down, forward, to the side. Even fucking backwards. They're pretty bad ass." Jack grins. "They can hover like a hummingbird, but their wings only flap thirty times a second, instead of seventy or something for a hummingbird. I don't remember the numbers exactly, but you get the idea. The <u>point</u>," I say, holding his eyes, "is they have <u>ease</u> in their power."

A grin spreads across Jack's face. He nods, like he gets it. It took me a few more years to really get it, after I first heard it, but my grandmother's dragonfly story marked the beginning of something new for me. That was when it first occurred to me that I could escape everything I'd been through, and that she could be the one to help me do it. And she was.

"The <u>best</u> part about dragonflies is they fly over the surface of the water, where everything's bright, without letting the deep, dark currents of their past touch them." Jack's expression grows more serious then. "Or hold them down."

"Yeah," he says quietly.

Somehow, I still don't know how, my grandmother helped me feel that for myself. It took her a while, but those years we lived with her changed me. I take a deep breath and smile, not really feeling the need to linger on the heaviness of everything. "Dragonflies have short lives, only a few months, so they live in the now."

Jack smiles too, following my lead. "Not a bad plan."

I nod. "Damn right. There will always be people who say living in the now is short-sighted and foolish," I say, echoing my grandmother's words, "but it's not." And the seriousness comes back without me meaning it to. "Because only in the <u>now</u> can we be present enough to know who we are. And only when we know who we really are can we make choices that are good for us without bumping into other dragonflies in the process."

I still remember how my grandmother said that, leaning forward and looking into my eyes. <u>No need to tear off our own wings in the process,</u> she'd said.

I was doing a whole hell of a lot of wing tearing those days, not just my own either.

Jack gives me a thoughtful look.

"I know this sounds corny or whatever," I say, smiling and shrugging, "but it's a cool idea. When dragonflies took on their true form, they gained unique beauty and effortless power."

"Leaving all that muck under the water."

"Exactly."

I smile and shrug, putting the dragonfly back in the box. "So that's kind of how it all started. You know, her helping me turn things around. She helped me see I didn't have to be my mother. Or my father. Or anyone. I could just be me and that's more than good enough. It's <u>awesome</u>."

Jack grins his big goofy grin and puts my grandmother's hat on his head.

"Be the dragonfly, and all that," he says nodding, the feather bobbing up and down. I laugh. This guy's a dragonfly himself, which is probably why I like him.

I dig into the box and pull out my grandmother's big clip-on earrings. They're gold medallions with huge pear-shaped faux pearls dangling down. I reach over to clip one on his ear and he holds still. I attach first one, then the other, and sit back to take him in.

He touches the earrings with both hands, then puts on a mock serious expression, jutting his chin into the air and striking a pose.

I laugh and start to pull out my phone so I can take a picture. "You're so pretty!"

He smiles, then catches sight of my phone.

"Oh no, you don't!" He yanks off the earrings too quickly and yelps.

"Wait! Just one!"

He flips off the hat and drops it in the box, scrambling to his feet.

"Come on, Instagram will love you!"

"Get away from me, woman!" He leaps over the box and darts away as the flowered scarf flutters to the floor.

Chapter 9

Sam

Ashley and Chloe are actually both here in the state at the same time, instead of off travelling somewhere, so everyone's over at my place for a girls' night. We spent the day shopping and getting pedis, and just finished dinner at El Toro. That's not stopping us from sitting around the kitchen island and digging into my collection of little Haagen Dazs containers. I bought them over a week ago, but I still have plenty, what with Jack being gone.

Stupid Spain.

Stupid Jack.

He finally got around to returning my texts and has kind of kept in touch. Every few days, I guess. I mean, it's fine. He's on vacation with his little woman and probably doesn't have time to text all day. Whatever. It's fine.

He's been there almost two whole weeks and I guess he would stay there fucking forever if he and <u>Emily</u> didn't have client meetings coming up and, you know, actual fucking work to do. He's been really vague about exactly when they're coming home, though. Hell if I know why. I haven't heard from him in a couple days. Whatever.

I take a bite of salted caramel gelato and listen as Chloe tells us about her and Grayson's upcoming travel itinerary. The website and YouTube channel they run together continues to rake in the dough, so they've got plenty of money to travel on.

Like Jack, I guess.

Stupid Jack.

When Chloe and Grayson first got engaged, she hinted that their busy schedule was keeping them from setting a date. But I think she's full of crap. I impulsively decide it's time to find out what's what.

"So why haven't you two set a date yet?" I ask her.

Chloe looks startled.

"Geez, Sam," Isabella says, rolling her eyes.

"What?" Chloe's looking down at her engagement ring. She's fiddling with it and wearing an uncomfortable expression. I can see she needs to talk about it. I think we need to stop tiptoeing around the topic. "You guys have been engaged for, like, two months now. What's the deal?"

She sighs and puts her spoon on the counter. Isabella, Ashley, and I all lean in slightly, waiting.

"Well," she starts. She gives us a sheepish look. "I'm kind of afraid to send out invitations."

"Ahhh," Ashley says, and we all sit back at once.

Well, that makes sense. Chloe's first fiancé called things off after they sent out like a billion invites, so I can see why she'd be hesitant. I once saw that asshole and the little hussy he'd been cheating on Chloe with at the grocery store. This wasn't long after he broke Chloe's heart, so I was still pretty pissed. Jack and I had been brainstorming revenge tactics, but I took my opportunity while I had it. I got out of the store before they saw me, found his car in the parking lot, and let the air out of all the tires. It was juvenile and not near as rotten as what he deserved, but it was satisfying anyway. I never mentioned it to Chloe, but Jack rewarded me with a fist bump when I told him.

I don't think I'd be keen to send out invitations either, if I were in Chloe's shoes. "So just elope then." I shrug. Easy enough.

"No, I still want the wedding. I guess I'm just being a little gun shy about it."

Isabella gives her a thoughtful look. "Are you having doubts about marrying Grayson?"

"Oh, no." Her face takes on a glow. "No, he's amazing. Wonderful. I love him so much."

"I'm going to puke," I say.

"No," Chloe continues, smiling at me and not missing a beat. "I already feel like I know we'll be together the rest of our lives, you know? I mean, you guys know what that feels like, right? To feel like you belong to someone?"

My heart starts thumping in this thick, agitated way.

I don't know why.

Stupid Spain.

Stupid Jack.

My phone rings at that exact moment, and it's Jack's ringtone.

My heart's still pumping hard. I think I'm just feeling badly for Chloe.

"Hey stranger," I answer lightly. I might be irritated with him, but I'm still glad to talk to him.

"Hey you." Wow. It's really good to hear his voice. "You home?"

"Yeah. The girls and I are eating ice cream without you. Sucker."

"Good to know."

Chloe grins, and Isabella hollers, "Hi Jack!"

"What's up?" I ask him.

"I just wanted to make sure you're home."

I suddenly realize why. "Are you back?"

The girls all straighten at this potentially good news, grinning and looking at me. My heart's really pumping. God, I feel really weird.

"Yeah," he says. "Can I stop by?"

"Why the fuck are you even asking?" I'm teasing, but not. <u>Just get over here already.</u>

"I don't know. I just wanted to make sure you're home."

Since when does he check? "Stop being weird. And you'd better hurry up if you want any ice cream. It's almost gone."

Isabella once asked me why Jack and I never hug.

I thought that was a really stupid question, until I thought about it.

I didn't realize it before, but we kinda don't. When he comes over, he'll hug and kiss all over the other girls, sure. But he and I will fist bump, or he'll jolt the tickle spot on my side like a big jerk, or we'll just kind of fall into each other's presence. I don't know. We don't need to hug, I guess.

"Why would I want to hug a dork like Jack?" I'd answered, teasing. Isabella just laughed and didn't push it. I didn't give it any more thought either.

Well, seeing Jack walk through my front door now, I feel like running up to him and giving him a big, big, big hug. It's a weird sensation. I don't get the chance to find out if I would've actually done it though, because in the next second, who should come through the door with him but a woman I can only assume is named Emily.

Well, the girls fall all over themselves with introductions and slyly examining Jack's new specimen. I'm doing a little examining of my own. He spent weeks in Spain with this woman and hasn't dumped her yet? What's the deal with this...

Um...

Okay, not a bimbo, I have to admit. She's in jeans and a cute, casual shirt and looks normal enough. Tall. Pretty.

I don't like her.

Why is she here? Why didn't Jack say he was bringing her?

"Hey Sam," he says, but he's not looking at me. As for Jack, Spain's been really good to him. He's tan and... has he been working out? I guess he looks like he always does, but for some reason I'm noticing the muscles in his arms and his chest. Must be the snug tee he's wearing that's drawing so much attention to his really pretty amazing-looking pecs. "Uh, this is Emily."

"Come on in," I say, trying to catch my feet. I don't know why I feel so thrown off. "There's ice cream in the kitchen, if you want some."

"Oh, thanks," she says, smiling right at me.

Ugh, her voice is so grating. Why are the girls all grinning ear to ear?

"We just had dinner though." She puts a hand on her stomach. "I'm stuffed."

Lightweight.

Jack's arm is around her waist and hers is around his. We're all just kind of standing around looking at each other—not that Jack will look at me—and my girls will not stop smiling at Emily.

I roll my eyes. "Well, have a seat, everyone."

That gets people moving. Why is everyone acting so weird? It's not like we've never met one of Jack's girls before. Not that I've ever met one here.

Which I'm kind of not happy about. Don't ask me why.

But I'm sure it won't be the last time I meet some chick he's dating.

Okay, yeah, this one's lasted awhile. But...

I frown.

Why has this one stuck around so long?

I sink into a chair and pull my feet up, folding my arms against my chest. Isabella starts asking Emily questions about herself, trying to get to know her, I guess.

Jack and Emily settle on one end of the couch. She leans against him and he hangs his arm over her shoulders, his hand hanging down. As Emily starts talking about what she does for work, Jack finally looks at me.

My heart starts pounding in this irritating way as we just look at one another. What's he doing? Why hasn't he been texting me?

He gives me a tentative smile and I feel pulled back into his orbit. I scrunch up my face at him. He kind of chuckles.

Emily must think he chuckled at something she said—she has this big, stupid smile on her face—because she just pats his knee as if to say, "I know, it's so funny!" and goes on with whatever she's saying. I'm not even listening.

I stick my tongue out at Jack and he grins.

I feel better for a moment.

Then Emily reaches up and grabs Jack's hand that's hanging by her shoulder. She laces her fingers through his and settles deeper against him.

The back of my neck tingles as I remember Jack's fingers rubbing me there. I grow still inside, just like I did when it happened. I remember being against his body, his face so close, that expression. What was it?

Jack and I are still looking at each other, but neither one of us are smiling.

My heart is beating faster, all light like wings.

Chapter 10

Jack

Don't think I don't know what I just did. I brought Emily into strict Firework Girls territory.

I've never once brought a girl I was dating into the Firework Girl Zone, wherever it was at the time. The girls would meet my current date at the bars, or the frat parties, or in the dorms, or on trips, or at the beach. But I've never brought a girl I was dating into the inner circle, like I did tonight.

I'm not sure why I did it. I missed my friends (Sam's only a friend, only a friend, only a friend) and I wanted to see them. That's not so weird, right? But hell if I was going to go over there without Emily. She's my life raft right now.

And isn't this what people do when they're advancing their relationships anyway? They introduce their girlfriends to friends and family. It's totally normal.

But all the work I did in Spain to distance myself emotionally from Sam?

Shot to hell the second I laid eyes on her.

Chapter 11

Sam

The girls <u>love</u> Emily. Fucking love her. After Jack and Emily left last night, Chloe could not stop talking about how <u>nice</u> she is and how <u>great</u> it is that Jack's found a nice girl.

Well, whatever. I'm not giving it a second thought.

I didn't sleep well last night for some reason, so I got up early and picked up several gallons of paint at Lowe's and sent texts to people (yeah, Jack too) saying if they felt up for a painting party to come on over. If not, fine. I have so much pent up energy, I feel like I could paint this whole damn house myself and not get tired.

I probably just need a good, solid orgasm or something, but I'm really not in the mood to go trolling for guys and I'm sick to death of these ugly green walls.

Jack shows up first. Alone. Thank God. I don't feel like dealing with Emily. I can't put my finger on what it is I don't like about her, but it bugs me that no one else can see it.

Anyway, Jack's in his old torn jeans and a faded, loose tee I haven't seen since college. The word sexy crosses my mind when I see him, but I push that kind-of-alarming thought away. I really, really need a normal day with my friend and it's bad enough that he's been weird lately. I'm not going to be stupid too.

"Is that your painting shirt?" I ask as he walks through the door, a couple six-packs in his hands. I'm up on the ladder, paint brush in hand, and already have paint on my shirt.

"Yeah." He gives me a big Jack grin that I don't mind admitting I've missed. "You move all this yourself, Shorty?" He's taking in the furniture I've pushed to the center of the room. I threw several plastic drop cloths over everything. I didn't bother protecting the pink shag carpeting, as its days are numbered anyway.

118

I nod. "What do you think of the color?" I gesture to the wall. It's a nice taupe, but the manufacturer unfortunately decided to call it 'Beavertail.' I almost eliminated it based on the stupid name of the color alone.

He frowns at the furniture. "Is your stomach okay? You should've waited for me to help you."

"My stomach's fine now and I didn't know if you were coming."

"Why wouldn't I come?" But the second he says it, he looks at me like he knows better. Things just haven't been the same with us lately, there's no getting around it. I wish I knew why. I miss him.

In fact, it's probably our recent time apart that's making him look all sexy right now, right? Makes sense. But I'm not going to think about that. I wave the paintbrush in the air, showing him the new color on the bristles. "Well?"

"Nice." He nods and heads for the kitchen. "That the beaver one?"

"Yeah," I say, as he disappears. I return to the wall in front of me and drop a thick line of color.

"I wondered which one you'd picked," he hollers. I take a deep breath, trying to get this weird unsettled feeling inside me to go away. "Want a beer?"

"Okay."

He comes in and hands one up to me. "Look at that, Shorty. You're actually taller than me." He gives me a big grin.

I roll my eyes and try not to encourage him with a smile, but I can't help it. "Shut up, Jack."

It's not long before things feel almost normal again. Man, it's so nice. We're laughing and joking and being silly and it's about damned time. I get Jack all to myself for two whole hours before other people start to show up to help. Isabella and Shane. A little later, Ashley and Erik. When we're done with the living room and almost done with the dining room, Chloe and Grayson show up even though she made the drive up from Swan Pointe just yesterday. I hadn't even included her in the texts this morning because I figured she wouldn't want to make the trip again. Turns out Ashley texted her.

Chloe says the drive up here is nothing compared to all the global travelling they do and is being her usual, bubbly self. By the time we're done for the day and waiting for pizza to arrive, she says she and Grayson have finally set a date to get married.

Everyone congratulates them and I'm proud of her for taking a step I know was scary. They've set the date for next spring, which Isabella declares gives them plenty of time to do all the crap people do for weddings. We've uncovered the furniture and pushed it back just enough to climb on, so we're all kind of cramped together. All the guys except Jack use the close quarters as an excuse to hang in the kitchen, but I think they're just trying to escape the wedding talk. The girls and Jack and I are sitting in a loose circle, with Jack opposite me in the chair.

Chloe's talking wedding venues and glowing and I'm genuinely happy for her, but then she goes and throws out this zinger:

"So is Jack going to be the next one to get married?" she says, teasing him.

And Jack? Well, he doesn't shudder or protest or anything.

Something inside me is suddenly cold.

He gets a really weird look, then laughs, shrugging it off, but it's not a normal Jack laugh.

"I really like her," Chloe says.

This again.

"Yeah, she's great," Jack says. Something in me twinges. "Really great."

It could be my imagination, but it seems he's back to not looking at me. All of a sudden I'm sick of whatever the hell's going on with him. Why can't he just be normal Jack? What's with all the weird vibes I've been getting from him for weeks and his strange behavior? Like the Spain thing. Something about that doesn't sit right with me.

Ashley's giving me a weird look. Come to think of it, she kept looking at me like this last night when Chloe and Isabella couldn't stop talking about the fabulous Emily.

Whatever. I don't have room in my brain to think about Ashley because Jack keeps talking. "She's got her stuff together, you know? She's got a good job. She's smart. She even has a five-year plan."

"Are you part of the plan?" Chloe says with a wink.

Shut up, Chloe.

Jack shrugs but he's not smiling. I can't read his expression at all. I'm so sick of this. "Maybe," he says. "I'd be lucky, right? She's really great."

"You said that already," I say. "Are you falling in love with this girl or shopping for a new car?"

Well, that got him to look at me. I look right back.

"What's that supposed to mean?" He's trying to play it cool. He's even giving me the benefit of the doubt and wearing a half grin, but I can see his irritation just under the surface. It only eggs me on.

"You're being so fucking analytical about it." His grin disappears in an instant. "It doesn't sound like there's any actual passion. Where's the spark?"

"Uh..." Chloe says hesitantly. They're all looking back and forth between Jack and I like they're watching a fucking tennis match. I don't care.

Jack's eyes are hard like flint. "Oh, there's a spark, don't you worry."

Grrrr. I just want to pound him. Don't ask me why. "Who the hell says I'm worried? You know, Jack, you should marry her. What the hell? With your spark and her five-year plan, you should just run right out and get her a ring."

"Maybe I will."

The others gape at him in shock. My chest feels like it's been caught in a vise.

Wait a minute. What did he just say?

"What?" he asks defensively, looking around at everyone's stunned expressions. "No one thinks Jack's marrying material, huh?"

"No one said that," Chloe says, taken aback.

"Jack just said it himself," I say, just to dig at him.

It worked.

"You're such a pain in the ass, Sam."

"Right back at you."

"What the hell did I do?"

"Oh, forget it." I get up and head for the kitchen. The men are cautiously drifting in from the kitchen though, drawn by our raised voices and blocking my way.

"You know what?" Jack says, and I turn enough to see him getting up too. I stop and fold my arms over my chest. "I'll see you guys later."

He stomps out the front door and slams it behind him. Three faces swing on me. Chloe and Isabella are gaping at me. Ashley's still giving me that weird look. Why is she looking at me like that?

"What the hell was that?" Isabella says.

Ashley says, "Sam, Jack was just—"

"Jack can kiss my ass." I march down the hall toward my room. I hear Jack's truck tear away, but I don't care. I don't need him.

I don't.

Everyone leaves me alone, and it's just as well. After storming around my bedroom for a while, I slowly start to cool down. After that, it doesn't take long for me to feel horrible. What the hell's the matter with me? Jack didn't deserve any of that.

I should go apologize to my poor guests, if they haven't slunk off by now, but first thing's first.

I send Jack a text: <u>I'm sorry. Really.</u>

After a minute he texts back. <u>Okay.</u>

I sigh. This isn't a texting sort of conversation. I want to apologize properly. If I call, will you answer?

Two minutes go by before my phone buzzes. <u>Okay.</u>

I call immediately.

He answers with a quiet, "Hey."

"Hey. Jack, I really am sorry. I don't know why I was being such a pain in the ass, but it was over the line."

He sighs.

I take a resolute breath and say what I know he needs to hear. "I think it's great." I pinch my eyes shut and concentrate really hard on making my voice sound sincere. "You and Emily. Really. It wasn't about that. It wasn't you. It was just..."

I'm rambling. I don't know what it was. I'm just a pain in the ass. Like he said.

"If you're happy, I'm happy. I just... I guess I just don't know Emily yet. But I'm sure I'll like her. I mean, you like her, right?"

I wonder if he's going to say he loves her and hope he doesn't.

"Yeah."

I'm gripping the phone and my heart is running ahead of time. I don't know why. Maybe I'm scared he's going to stay mad at me. Not that I don't deserve it.

"Are we still friends?" I ask. "Do you forgive me?"

There's a bit of a pause. "I <u>suppose</u>," he says with an exaggerated sigh.

I unclench a bit. He forgives me.

"But try to keep your head out of your ass in the future."

I press my lips together. This is the revenge part of him accepting my apology.

"Uh-huh," I say, taking my lickings.

"And next time you're on the rag, steer clear of me until you're done, okay?"

Boy, he's really going for the jugular. Jack knows perfectly well how much I <u>hate</u> it when asshole guys blame stuff on a woman's period.

"Uh-huh."

"And Sam?"

"Yeah?" I'm waiting for the last bomb to drop.

This time the pause goes on so long, I'd think he hung up if I couldn't hear the connection. "We'll always be friends."

This pains me more than it seems it should.

"I..." I begin. I really hurt. I don't know why. "I guess it has kind of felt like... I've been losing my friend. I guess I was being selfish."

He doesn't answer. He's so quiet.

"I really am sorry I was such an ass."

"Well," he says in his teasing voice, "who can blame you? Who'd want to lose a fantastic friend like me?"

"Okay." I roll my eyes, but I'm smiling.

"I mean, how could you possibly go on without me?"

The smile slides off my face. My chest is aching again.

"Okay." But I think I'm done talking now. "Goodbye, Jack."

"Goodbye, Sam."

That night, I have a dream.

A dream about Jack.

It starts on my couch. We're watching a movie but I don't recognize whatever's on the screen. I'm against his chest and his arm is around me. His fingers are brushing the back of my neck, caressing it so softly. I rub my hand up his chest. It's firm and warm. My body is tingling all over, just from touching his chest and him touching my neck.

I turn my head to look up at him. His arm tightens around me. He looks me in the eye as he leans in and puts his lips on mine. Warm and soft. My heart swoops up into my throat.

Things change then.

We're kissing, really kissing, tongues eager. He's on top of me and we're in my bed. I'm fully dressed but he only has jeans on. My hands are all over his bare back and my legs are tight around his waist. His hard length digs into me and I'm so, so eager for him.

Things change again.

His cock's in me and we're both naked and sweating. He's kissing me like he can't get enough and squeezing my breasts.

My body is climbing and climbing. It goes on and on. Jack inside me and my heart bursting open and my body aching for release. I get so close. Again and again I'm almost there as I feel him rubbing inside me, but I never go over.

My agitation pulls me into a state of partial dreaming, partial awareness. Part of me knows it's a dream, but part of me still thinks it's real and so damned good. My body is squirming in bed. The part of me that knows it's a dream understands that's the reason why I haven't been able to come. The dream hangs on, Jack still fucking me, and he feels so amazing and I want him so much. The real me slides my hand under my panties, barely aware of what I'm doing. The second my finger touches my clit, I climax at last, contracting under the covers.

After a few seconds, my body releases and I'm left with a pounding heart. As the dream slides away, I realize where I am and what's just happened.

Then it hits me.

Oh my god, it all hits me. "Oh, god," I say aloud.

I love him.

"Oh, shit."

I'm in love with him.

The revelation is so powerful, I feel like it's flat knocked me over. And I'm fucking still lying in bed.

Suddenly, it all becomes horribly clear, what the unsettled feeling has been and why I've been so mad at him.

"No, no, no."

This can't happen. I can't fall in love with Jack. I can't fall in love with anybody. How the hell did this happen? It's his stupid fault for making me trust him and being all funny and sexy and freaking Jack. That boy snuck right under my radar and now I'm sunk.

Then I remember there's an Emily. My heart hurts so much I think it's going to stop beating. Now I know what I don't like about her.

Oh, god.

For a moment I wonder if I can hatch some sort plot to get rid of her. But I can't come up with a devious plot without my plotting partner, and my plotting partner is fucking Jack.

"Shit."

And even if I did get rid of Emily... or she got hit by a bus... or something... what then? I don't know the first thing about being in love. What? Do I, like, want to be in a relationship with Jack? What the hell would that even look like?

I have no clue. But I know how it would end. Like every bad relationship my mother's ever been in. Including, probably, her most current one.

No, no, no. I could never let that happen to me and Jack. Because you can't just go back to being friends after a tragedy like that. No, after relationships turn sour, you take to despising the person you used to love and the thought of despising Jack makes my heart hurt.

132

It makes my entire body hurt.

Every muscle in my body is clenched. I'm gripping the covers under my chin. I may as well be hiding from a boogeyman, the way I'm acting.

It <u>feels</u> like something's about to get me.

I love Jack and that terrifies me. It kills me to think I can't have him—what with the whole   we're-best-friends-and-he's-got-stupid-Emily thing—but I'm terrified to want him, too.

Except that I do.

Against all reason, I want him, want him, want him.

I close my eyes and pull the covers over my head.

"Fuuuuuuuck."

Chapter 12

Jack

I'm lying on the couch in Emily's condo, with Emily lying half next to me, half on top of me. We're watching <u>Grey's Anatomy</u>. I have my arms around her, because I'm allowed to do things like that with my girlfriend. It's only eight o'clock, but I think I'll head home soon. It's a work night, so that can be my reason. The real reason is things have been a little strained between Emily and me lately.

It's completely my fault, of course. I don't know what the fuck I'm doing any more. I really don't. Here I've got this great girl who actually wants me, but I'm busy wishing for the girl I can't have and fucking up my friendship with her to boot.

It's tearing me up.

I thought I could get this thing with Sam under control. I made progress in Spain. Kind of. Maybe it wasn't long enough. Maybe I shouldn't have come back. Do I need to move the fuck away forever? What do I need to do? Because with Sam in the same city, I can't seem to stay away. And all that does is make me want her more.

You'd think our fight would've helped, but no. It didn't. Because I've barely talked to Sam about Emily at all, and yet she knows me so well she hit the nail on head without hardly trying. That's probably what pissed me off more than anything.

I am being analytical about Emily. She's great. She really, really is. But even though everything about her and I together looks good on paper, my brain can't convince my heart to go along with it.

My heart wants Sam. My body wants Sam. Every time I see that girl I want to eat her the fuck up, but I can't. It's be her friend or nothing, because she's clearly not going to break her relationship rule just for me.

The way she scooted away from me on the couch that day still fucking hurts.

It's starting to feel like I have two choices: stay here and be miserable forever, or leave altogether and try to get to the point where I can at least breathe.

Emily readjusts and nuzzles deeper into me. She's getting heavy and a bit warm. Falling asleep, I think. Maybe if I move away, I can persuade Emily to come with me. Maybe it'll be easier to fall in love with her— because she really is a great girl—if I get clear of Sam.

I know I told Sam we'd always be friends. But that girl is breaking my heart.

My phone rings, causing Emily to stir. I reach over and grab it off the coffee table. The caller ID says "Nick Bartender." He's the main bartender over at Rounders. We usually only chat when I'm at the bar, but he's invited me to his house a few times for BBQs and his killer Super Bowl Parties. I didn't know his last name when I first put him in my phone. Thus, "Nick Bartender."

"Hey Nick," I answer. "What's up?"

"Hey Jack." His voice sounds serious. "This might be kind of weird, but I think you need to come down here and check on Sam."

"Sam? She's there?"

It's a Monday night. What's she doing at Rounders unless...

<u>Fuck, Nick.</u> I don't need to know every time Sam's down there picking up some guy.

Emily stirs again and lifts her head off my chest to look at me. I try to give her an "everything's fine" smile to get her to lie back down, but she's listening now.

"Yeah," Nick continues, "and she's so drunk I had to cut her off." Huh? Sam never gets drunk. <u>Ever</u>. "I don't really want to ask Frank to escort her out of here, but it's getting to that point. I don't know. I thought maybe...."

"Yeah," I say, watching as Emily's brows turn down. "No, I get it. Thanks. I'll be there soon."

Emily starts to crawl off me and sit up. I sit up, too. She's watching me like a hawk.

"Thanks, Jack," Nick says.

I get off the couch and slide my phone into my pocket, avoiding Emily's eyes.

"What was that about?" she asks as I go to the door and start putting on my shoes.

"Um..."

Okay, yeah, I'm having a hard time looking Emily in the eye at this precise moment, but let's be clear about something. Emily's not the jealous type, and I'm not the cheating type.

In fact, I think guys who cheat are stupid, selfish, bastards, but hey. Maybe that's just me.

That said, I'm perfectly aware that something in me is being a little evasive. "Sounds like Sam might be in a bit of trouble down at Rounders."

"She's at a bar on a Monday night? What kind of trouble?"

"Too much to drink, is all. I'll check on her on my way home. It's getting time for me to go anyway."

"Okay." But she's frowning a bit. She gets off the couch and comes over to give me a hug. When I take her into my arms, she leans her head on my shoulder and stays there for a while.

Okay, maybe I'm not technically doing anything wrong, but I'm starting to feel like the world's biggest ass.

I tuck my fingers under her chin and turn her to face me so I can kiss her. I try to give her the kind of kiss she deserves. It must not have been too bad, because when we pull away, she's smiling up at me.

I should be grateful a woman like her is smiling at me like that.

I give her a soft peck. "Call you tomorrow."

Then I head out the door, to get Sam.

Once I flash Frank my ID and make it inside Rounders, I do a quick scan and come up short. I spot Nick behind the bar and we make eye contact. He's pouring vodka into a glass, but nods in the direction of the back rooms.

Sam and I don't generally go back there unless we're playing pool or something, but maybe she has a different routine when she's here for... other reasons.

Ugh.

When I find her, she's in the narrow hallway that leads to the bathrooms, and is surrounded by three guys. I can't tell which one, if any, she has her sights on, because she's got her hand on one guy's chest but is smiling seductively—overtly so—at another. They all look like they're hoping to get lucky, which gets my blood boiling. She's dressed for it, too. She's wearing her tiny black skirt and black, laced suede boots that go up to her mid-thigh. I haven't seen those things in years.

As I approach, she's unsteady on her feet. Her body movements are exaggerated and unnatural. Yeah, she's clearly had a few too many. Whatever she's drinking, the glass in her hand is nearly empty.

One of the guys says something and she laughs, too loudly. God, it's really weird seeing her like this.

"Hey there, Sam."

Her eyes swing in my direction and fumble around a bit before landing on me and staying there. Her face lights up. "Jack!" She half walks, half stumbles in my direction, grinning and saying "Oh, Jack! Hi!"

She throws her arms around my waist and gives me an unbalanced hug. I hang on to her to keep her from falling. Also, just because. She's pressed all the way against me and I might be an asshole but she feels really, really good in my arms.

Still hanging on to me, she looks up and gives me a smile that I feel ballooning up in my chest. I smile back down at her. I'm really trying not to, but I fucking love her so much. Then she furrows her brows together. "Hey wait," she says loosely, "I'm mad at you."

"Again?"

She pushes herself off my chest, fumbling a bit with her nearly empty glass, the brown liquid swirling around in the base. She's fumbling with her feet too, for that matter. I hold her elbow to steady her. "I don't know," she says, frowning. "Did we make up?"

"I thought we did." I can't help but grin at her. She's so damned cute.

Her frown deepens as she looks back up at me, like she's trying to remember. "Oh no, no, no," she says in her ornery tone, turning back and heading for the guys, who've been doing their own bit of scowling in my direction. "I remember. I'm mad at you and your fingers."

Huh?

"So run along now." She twiddles her fingers in the air, half leaning against, half falling into the guy who had his arm around her before. He puts his arm around her again, his hand dangerously close to her ass. He gives me a satisfied smirk, but he's a moron if he thinks he's winning this battle. No fucking way am I leaving her like this. With him or anyone.

"Come on, honey." I reach out to her. "Let me take you home."

She shakes her head firmly and downs the rest of her drink in one fell swoop. "Be a doll and get me another one, would you, Chad?" She hands him the glass and smiles at him with half-lidded eyes.

Be a doll? Wow, her flirting really suffers when she's drunk. Still, Chad holds out the empty glass to one of his companions, who swaps it for a full one, which he then gives to Sam. Now I see how she's working around Nick's drink cap. Assholes.

"Hey," I say firmly, as she starts to drink up, but begins to lose her balance doing it. The guys laugh, watching her recover. "You've had enough, Sam."

"Back off, dude," Chad says.

I ignore him, coming right up and taking the glass from her. She makes a grab for it but I hold it out of reach. Chad straightens and puffs up his chest. I give him a murderous look that means business. He hesitates, sizing me up. Just try me, buddy.

"Hey!" Sam protests as I shove her glass toward another guy, who takes it just in time to keep it from spilling all over him. "I want more." She's practically pouting.

"No way. You've had enough."

She huffs and scowls at me. "You know, Jack, if you're going to ride my ass, you should at least pull my hair."

Even pissed as I am, even drunk as she is, my dick responds to the idea of riding her ass and pulling her hair. Fucking hell.

I take her hand, but she yanks it away. "Uh-uh, you. I'm going home with this one here," she says, jerking a thumb in Chad's direction.

This looks like news to him, but he smiles at her in a way that makes me want to knock his teeth out.

"Isn't that right, Chad?" she asks, but she's not looking at Chad. She's scowling at me.

Chad exchanges grins with one of the other guys. They're all grinning ear to ear. "Anything you want, baby. We'll take you home."

Yeah. I don't think so.

"I'm not leaving you here for a gang bang," I say, glaring at Chad, who narrows his eyes. I try to take her hand again, but she pulls back, scowling.

"You don't own me, Jack Thomas Anderson."

The guys laugh, but I ignore them. I'm done fucking around. I bend over, heft Sam over my shoulder, and turn back toward the main bar—Chad has to duck to keep her legs from hitting him in the face as I swing her around.

"Jack! Hey! Put me down!"

Her boots kick and her little fists pound on my back a couple times but I keep walking.

"Put me down right now or I'll puke all over your jeans!"

"They'll wash," I say, raising a hand to Nick, who's watching the whole thing and laughing.

"Jack, put me down!"

On the way out, I wave to the bouncer.

"See ya, Jack," he says. "Bye, Sam."

"Frank!" Sam hollers at him. "Frank, help me!"

Apparently she realizes Frank's not going to come to her rescue, because she says, "Ugh!" and flops down against my back.

I walk up to my truck, set her on wobbly legs, and open the passenger door. "Get in."

She folds her arms and scowls up at me. We stand there in silence, sizing each other up. She's getting in that truck if I have to toss her in myself.

She huffs and turns toward the seat. She's trying to climb in, but can't seem to aim her foot properly. I put my hand under her arm to help steady her, but she bats it away.

"I can do it myself."

I sigh and let go, but after she practically falls backward trying to lift her foot again, I catch her deftly and set her on the seat.

"See?" she says. "I told you I could do it."

"Yes, yes, you're a big girl," I mutter, shutting the door and going around to the driver's side.

By the time I buckle her in and start heading for her house, some of the fight seems to have gone out of her. She's leaning back, wedged between the seat and the door, her knees together and her feet angled out in opposite directions. We drive in silence for a while, which suits me fine because I'm catching my breath from the whole thing. What on earth is going on with her? I can't believe I just had to haul Sam out of a bar like that.

Thank God Nick called me. The thought of her going home with those snakes makes my blood boil. She never would've been even talking to guys like that if she weren't so smashed.

I look at her, leaning back in the seat and frowning out the window. Why _is_ she so smashed? My heart softens as I wonder if something horrible's happened to push her to drink like this.

"Any reason why you're drunk off your ass on a Monday night?" Or any night?

She lifts one foot and puts her boot on the dash, stretching out her leg. My eyes linger on her, my heart starting to pump. "This is all your fault."

"How is it my fault?"

She brings up the other leg and rests it on the dash as well. My cock responds to the sight of her lounging all over the seat and I face forward, squeezing the wheel. "I'm mad at you, Jack."

Well, that's helpful. I already know she's mad at me. Again. Hell if I know why.

"I'm going to throw up."

I look over sharply, wondering if I have time to pull over. She's leaning back, legs still stretched out, staring out the windshield with a somber expression. Of course it can be hard to tell, but she doesn't look about to throw up. I take my chances and keep driving.

There's a minute of silence, then, "Where's <u>Emily?</u>"

I squeeze the wheel. "Home."

"Do you love her, Jack?"

"Uh—" I say, caught off guard by her question. I'm saved having to answer though, because she goes on.

"I bet you do. What's not to love? She's beautiful and smart and funny and tall. How tall is she?"

"Five ten."

"What?! Holy hell. See? You only have three inches on her. I once had sex with a guy who was six five. Remember him. What was his name?"

"Hell if I know."

"It was odd, too, because his pecker was kinda tiny. We made it work though."

"God, Sam."

"Hey, how many girls have you made fall in love with you?"

I look at her sharply again. Say what? "I don't make girls fall in love with me." <u>If I could, I wouldn't be in this fucking mess.</u>

"Let's see, there was Trisha," she says, counting off on her fingers, "and, uh, that blonde one. What the hell was her name?" She puts up another finger. "And Sharice." Three fingers. "Remember that girl? She had the great big hair." She holds her hands out from her head to indicate.

When she brings her hand back in front of her, she's not holding up her fingers anymore. She frowns. "Wait, how many was that?"

"Do you have a point over there?"

"Yeah. You totally shouldn't make girls fall in love with you. It's kinda crappy. I mean, what if someone doesn't <u>want</u> to be in love with you?"

"Well, no one <u>has</u> to fall in love with me. Geez, Sam."

"Ha!" she says loudly, pointing at me.

I stare at her. <u>What the hell?</u>

She falls back against the seat and takes to looking out the windshield. "Shows what you know."

I go back to staring at the road. "You're so fucking drunk," I mumble.

"Meh. I'm really mad at you, Jack."

"Yeah, well, I'm mad at you, too."

She frowns, apparently confused. "What did I do?"

I don't answer and she doesn't talk any more either.

By the time I get her home and am helping her into her bedroom, she's mellowed and so have I. I'd let her just pass out on her bed fully dressed, but she's got these long, freaking boots on.

I sit her on the edge of the bed and kneel in front of her, looking for the end to those laces that zig zag all the way up the front. I'm trying really hard not to look at the base of her short skirt and the dark triangle of shadow there. She's a bit unsteady, even sitting, and has a hand on each of my shoulders. I imagine her putting her hands on the back of my head and pressing me in closer to that dark triangle—I can't help it— and my dick throbs in response. Fuck.

"Ugh," I say, giving up on the damned boots. "How the hell do you get these things off?"

"There's a thing." She points. She lifts the top of a black suede flap that runs down the length of the boot. "A thing," she says again, then I see it.

"Oh, a zipper."

"Yeah."

"That's clever." Thank God, because I'm in no mood to deal with all that lacing. I pull on the zipper and start to question the wisdom of this plan. As the boot opens up to reveal more and more of Sam's bare leg, the crotch of my jeans gets uncomfortably tight.

As I start to pull off the first boot, she tries standing to help make things easier. Even though her hands are still on my shoulders, she wobbles again. I grab her by the hips to keep her from falling, then gently set her back down. "God, Sam," I say softly. "Why'd you drink so much?"

One hand absently caresses my shoulder and runs down my bicep. Holy hell.

"I fucked up," she says quietly. "I didn't mean to."

I sigh. I'm unzipping the other boot and looking at that soft skin and telling myself under absolutely no circumstances can I caress her leg. Or do any of the other naughty things I'm dying to do to her.

"I didn't mean to," she says again.

"Okay, honey. You're all right. You'll have a fun time working this one off, though." I grab the boots and lean away a bit so I can toss them near the closet.

Her hands grip my shoulders. "Don't leave me, Jack."

"I'm not. I'm just putting your boots over here."

Then Sam slides off the bed and onto my lap, her arms around my neck and her head tucked onto my shoulder. "I don't want to be alone."

My heart is pounding. Part of me wonders what on earth happened to her to make her act like this, and the other part of me—selfishly, like a bastard—is grateful for whatever it is because I'm holding Sam in my lap and she feels so, so good. She smells so good.

She squeezes me and I squeeze her back. I rub my hand down her side and to her waist. I force myself to freeze, because I don't want to stop there. I don't want to stop there at all.

Because apparently I'm the kind of guy willing to think about taking advantage of his best friend when she's completely smashed.

I have to put the brakes on things right now. "Time to get some sleep." I get to a stand with her in my arms, then lay her on her side. No fucking way am I taking off the skirt. She'll just have to deal with it.

"Stay," she whispers, her eyes closing as she starts to settle into the pillow.

"You're okay now."

"Stay." She takes my hand and grips it hard. "Please, Jack. Please."

"Alright." I'm helpless to say anything else when she's pleading so pitifully like that. What in the hell happened to her? When she sobers up, I'll try to find out. "Alright," I say again.

Eyes still closed, she sighs and rolls onto her back.

"Oh, no you don't." I turn her onto her side again. I don't need this girl choking on her own vomit. I don't know if she's passed out or fallen asleep already, but her hand drops out of my hand and she starts snoring softly.

I exhale heavily and stand up, looking down at her. My blood is pumping thickly and I'm having a hard time getting my Johnson to settle down. I bring my hands to my face, rubbing hard. Would I be a complete ass if I jacked off in her bathroom?

Instead, I go back into the living room to lock up the house. I empty my pockets onto the kitchen counter and look for the extra charger I keep here so I can plug in my phone. I realize just how much I've made a home for myself here at Sam's. I really should cut those strings. Draw firmer boundaries.

I consider sleeping on the couch, but it's too short for comfort. I kind of want to keep an eye on Sam anyway, and my cock is finally under control. Sort of. I go back into her bedroom to see she's rolled onto her back again, her arms and legs spread out.

Don't look, don't look, don't look.

I manage not to look <u>too</u> much at the black lace panties I can see under her skirt. Good lord, is she wearing a <u>thong?</u> So much for my cock being under control.

Dammit Sam.

I focus on turning her onto her side again. It kind of worries me that she won't stay put. Sam's a wild sleeper.

I pull the covers down and tuck her under them (panties safely out of sight). Her shoulders are still showing though, and her shoulders are sexy as hell. I pull the blankets up more, covering them. Then up a bit more, covering her neck. Okay. That's better. Kind of.

I strip down to my boxers and tee and collapse on the other side of the bed, on top of the covers. My dick is demanding some attention, but thankfully my exhaustion wins over. I'm out in a heartbeat.

I keep waking up. Between worrying about her and waking to check to make sure she hasn't choked in her sleep, and her rolling all over the place and throwing her limbs all over me, I'm not sleeping much.

It's my own fucking fault. I should've just left.

I realize this keenly when, predawn, I wake to find Sam in my arms, and me in hers. We're on our sides, facing each other, arms wrapped around one another. Her leg is thrown over my hip and she's oh-so-slowly grinding against my hard cock. Her skirt has scrunched up in her sleep and she's definitely, definitely wearing a thong. I know this because my hand is low on her bare ass. Half an inch lower and I'll be fingering the gateway to heaven. She's still sleeping, and making dreaming noises, but now I'm wide awake. She's probably dreaming about some random hookup, but I'm right here, right now.

She's pressed against my chest and nuzzling her mouth into the crook of my neck. Good lord. My heart's pounding against my ribs and I'm so hard it almost

156

hurts. I should move my hand off her ass, but I leave it there. It's taking every ounce of self-control not to roll her on her back, tear that black lace thong right off her, and pound her into oblivion.

Fucking hell.

I scramble backwards out of bed. She kind of moans but I don't look to see if I woke her up. I will lose it if I stay here another second, and I know it. I hustle into the living room, throw on my clothes, and get the hell out.

It's only after I've made it home and let off some steam in the shower that I'm clear-headed enough to realize what might be the worst thing:

I didn't leave out of loyalty to Emily.

I left out of loyalty to Sam.

Chapter 13

Sam

If I don't stop having these stupid dreams about Jack, I'm going to lose my fucking mind. Or, alternately, my head could just explode and put me out of my misery. Why oh <u>why</u> do people drink like this?

I barely remember last night. I'm not sure how I got home, but the fact that I'm still dressed is a good sign. My car's not here though. Is it down at the bar? I keep thinking Jack was there, and here, but I'm not sure if that was part of my dream or what.

I called in sick to work. In case you're wondering, calling in sick to work due to a drinking binge is officially fucked up behavior. Dear ol' dad would be so proud.

Fuck.

Around noon I stumble out to the kitchen to make some coffee and text Jack.

Me: Did you bring me home last night?

Jack: You=wasted. Me=awesome.

I groan.

Me: Where's my car?

Jack: Rounders. We can get it later. Did you call into work?

Me: What do you think?

Jack: Are you okay?

Me: <u>Yeah.</u>

Jack: I mean really.

I groan again. No, Jack, you big, dumb, jackass I am most definitely not okay.

Me: Yes really. Except my head is no longer attached to my body.

Jack: You weren't using it anyway.

"You got that right, buddy."

I don't want Jack to help me get my car because I don't think I can handle being with him. I call Ashley. Then I call Isabella. Then the next thing I know, Chloe's hauled herself clear up to Rosebrook yet again because I've called an emergency meeting at Delsa's Diner. We take my car home, then go to Delsa's together in Isabella's car.

We're sitting in our spot, near the back. This was the first place we ever hung out together, way back in our Freshman year, and it hasn't changed one bit. The floors are still white linoleum, and the booths are still cheap red leather, and the menu is exactly the same. But we're all different. I'm different.

I didn't think I could handle Volcano Fries, so I ordered one of Delsa's famous cookie pies and the girls all jumped on board. We each have an individual cookie pie in front of us, with a couple scoops of ice cream on top.

I know I'm the one who called this little meeting, but now that everyone's here, what am I supposed to say? What are they supposed to do about it? I'm stabbing my ice cream with my spoon, but I'm not eating it.

"Are you going to tell us what's wrong, or what?" Chloe asks.

"I guess. What the hell." But I still say nothing.

Isabella snorts. "Geez, Sam."

"I know. I'm being a pain in the ass."

That's part of what's bugging me, too. I never realized it before, but part of not wanting to ever fall in love was not having to worry about being loveable. I mean, what hope does a pain in the ass like me have anyway?

"Um," Ashley says, frowning at me. "What's that look about? You look like you're in a really dark place."

Okay, I just have to come out with it. But as I think about telling them the truth, that I've gone and fallen in love with Jack when I shouldn't have, a bubble of pain is swelling in my chest. I tilt my head up slightly, blinking back tears. Oh God. The Heartbreak. I've tried so hard to avoid this. I don't want this. I don't.

"Oh, Sam," Isabella says softly. "What is it?"

I drop my spoon and clasp my hands together, pressing them hard against my forehead. Now I do want to spill it all and tell them everything, but I don't think I can physically talk. I'm fighting back a sob and can only spit out, "Jack," before I break down and start crying right here in the middle of fucking Delsa's Diner.

"Jack?" Chloe repeats. "Is something wrong with him?"

"Yeah, he's in love with fucking Emily, that's what's wrong with him," I say, looking up. "Stupid asshole."

Chloe and Isabella look alarmed and confused—and who can blame them—but Ashley is giving me a more compassionate look. As if she understands. I realize she's probably understood this for some time. I'm such an idiot.

"Oh, Sam," Ashley says.

"What?" Chloe asks, looking between the two of us.

I grab a napkin and furiously wipe away my tears, leaving trails of mascara on the white tissue. "I've gone and fallen in love with stupid Jack, that's what."

Chloe slams both hands on the table and lowers her head, staring at me. "Whaaaat?"

Isabella's jaw drops.

162

"Uuuugh," I groan. "I know, I know. We're supposed to be friends and he's with Emily anyway and I'm so <u>sick </u>of hearing him swoon over that little princess."

"I don't know that I'd call it swooning," Isabella mutters, shrugging, but Chloe's still staring at me in disbelief.

"You fell in love with Jack?" she says.

"I didn't mean to!"

"Okay," Isabella says. "It's okay."

But Chloe's not done. She looks at Ashley. "Did you know about this?"

"Not exactly."

"What's that mean?" Chloe presses.

"It means I kinda figured it out."

Chloe is furrowing her brows at Ashley but I don't care who knew what or who figured out what. Although, I'm a little perturbed by the notion that Ashley may have figured it out before I did.

"Okay, everybody calm down," Isabella says. "Does Jack know?"

"Are you fucking crazy?" I say.

"I was <u>just</u> <u>asking</u>," she says, raising her hands.

I groan and drop my head in my hands. "Sorry, Bella." She sighs and starts rubbing my back. "I don't know what to do," I say, my head still in my hands. "This is so, so, so bad."

"Well," Ashley says slowly, "maybe Jack feels the same way?"

I look at her wryly. Typical, female wishful thinking. And dammit if I don't start up with it, too. I've thought of that night plenty. But I'm still giving her a look. She holds her ground. "He might."

I glance at the other two. They're giving Ashley thoughtful looks.

"He's with Emily," I say, determined to be logical about this. "The first girl he's never cringed about when someone brings up the topic of marriage."

Chloe cringes herself. Everyone exchanges uncomfortable looks. Because I'm right.

"Uggggh," I say again, sliding down and resting my head on the back of the seat. "This just.... ugh... I can't stand this! How can you people stand this?"

Chloe laughs a little.

"It's so not fucking funny," I say flatly, pinching my eyes closed.

It's silent at our table for a moment. There's a song playing on the jukebox: "I Will Always Love You," by Whitney Houston. Nice. Whatever.

"How long have you felt like this?" Isabella asks.

I shrug, like a petulant teenager.

"Sam?" she presses.

I sigh and sit back up. "I don't know. Not long. I don't think. It just... all kind of hit me. I had a...dream about him." I feel my cheeks blushing, and let me tell you, it's been years since I've been embarrassed about anything sexual.

Chloe's eyebrows raise and I point at her. "Don't say anything." She widens her eyes and raises her hands, pretending she wasn't going to.

"And then..." I continue, "I think, I don't know, maybe because Emily came on the scene? I don't know. I don't know where all this came from."

"Honestly," Isabella says gently, "I never understood why you two weren't an item to start with."

Well, great. What am I supposed to do with that?

"Has Jack ever given you any sign that he might feel the same way?" Isabella asks.

And here I go again. I think back to that night weeks ago. Movie night. Fingers on my neck and goosebumps on my arms night. The way he looked at me. Remembering makes my heart hurt.

"It was nothing," I say aloud.

They all straighten and lean in. "What's this?" Chloe says.

"Nothing," I say, irritated now. "No. There has not been anything and Jack is not hiding secret feelings for me."

I'm not going to be one of those women who analyzes every little thing a guy does so she can convince herself he's in love with her.

"Sam," Ashley says firmly, "I'm sorry, but you don't_know that. You have all these feelings for Jack now, right? Have you ever done anything to show it? Does <u>he </u>have anything he could look at and say, Gee, I think Sam likes me?"

That gets me thinking, I'll admit. It's a fair point. Maybe.

"You need to talk to him," she says.

My eyes widen and I give my head two sharp shakes no. Uh-uh. No way. I'm panicking just at the thought of it.

"You need to," Ashley says.

"Maybe she's right," Isabella pipes in.

Fuck. "No. No, I can't." That panicked feeling is growing. "I can't lose him." I mean his friendship, but I don't clarify.

"Hey," Ashley says gently, as I take a deep breath. This conversation is freaking me out. "Even if Jack doesn't feel the same way, he's not going to stop being your friend. You know he won't."

"I'll make it weird. It'll ruin it. That's what happens."

"You and Jack are different," Isabella says. "You'll work through it."

I throw my hands up. "Well, what's the point? Why do I want to give him something to work through?"

I just need to fucking get over it. And I'm not going to be one of those women who thinks she's the exception. I'm not, or else he... he wouldn't be with Emily the way he is. My heart clenches in pain as I think about Emily. The girl he loves. Not me. Her. And as much as I hate to admit it, she deserves him more than I do. She's smart and beautiful and has her shit together and probably isn't a miserable fuck-up in the love department like I am.

"Sam—" Isabella starts to press.

I cut her off. "Anyway, who says I want him?"

They all stare at me.

"You don't want him?" Chloe asks.

"I don't... want to want him."

"That's just stupid," Isabella says, taking a bite of her cookie.

"No, it's not." Some help they're being.

"You want him," Isabella says. "You're just scared he doesn't want you."

"Or scared he does," Ashley says.

I look at Ashley sharply. My heart's pounding. I take a few steadying breaths, then say, "That's enough." I look at each one of them. "That's enough. I'm done talking about it."

For better or for worse, no one says another word.

Chapter 14

Sam

Isabella drops me off and I enter a darkened house. It was daylight when the girls picked me up earlier, and I forgot to turn on any lights before I left. I shut the door behind me and stand there in the dark, my purse hanging loosely from my hand. I don't move. I don't think. I just stand there.

After a moment I reach over and flip the switch next to the door. The floor lamp in the corner comes on. I stare at the living room. The walls are taupe instead of puke green. The furniture is back where it belongs, for now. The pink shag carpet is still awaiting its fate.

I drop my purse on the floor, step out of first one heel, then the other, then walk barefoot down the darkened hall to my bedroom. Yellow light from the streetlamp outside is coming through the open blinds. I don't bother turning on any other lights. I strip off my jeans and throw them on the floor. My shirt and bra are next.

I open a drawer, grab a cami, and slowly pull it on. I remove a pair of old sweats from the same drawer and pull those on, too. I stare at the open drawer for a minute, then leave the room without closing it.

I go down the hallway and back into the living room where I stop and stand there. Just... stand there. Something dark is starting to seep into my shoulders and chest. It soaks into me, getting stronger. Going deeper.

I'm standing still, but yet I stumble a bit. I sink to the end of the coffee table, sitting heavily.

The blackness is starting to break open and pool inside my heart.

Oh god. No.

I can't remember what girls do when they're brokenhearted. What am I supposed to do? What do I do with this? How do I stop it?

But whatever horrible thing has been creeping up on me isn't creeping anymore, it's tearing through me. Without mercy. I hunch over and press my palms to my eyes. It swells and breaks inside me and just like that I'm crying like a child.

Make it stop. Make it stop. Make it stop.

But it goes on and on. I forgot what it was like to cry this hard and this long. Why did I do this to myself? How could I have let this happen? And with Jack. My best friend.

I don't know how long I'm like that. Eventually, I'm lying on the coffee table, staring up at the ceiling and feeling still and lifeless.

Naturally, that's when Jack walks in the door.

He takes one look at me and freezes, door still half way open and his hand still on the knob. I stay where I'm at. In the space of a heartbeat, I take Jack in. Tall, lean, handsome Jack. I've always known Jack's good looking, but it's one thing to see that with your eyes and another to have your entire body and soul react to it. It isn't just how he looks though, it's who he is and who he's always been to me. My truest friend.

It feels like there's a string attached to my heart, and Jack's got a hold of the other end, and he's pulling, pulling, pulling. Reeling me in.

"Um…" he says.

I roll my eyes. Oh my god, <u>what?</u> I guess when I texted "I'm going out with the girls" I should've said "I don't want to see you tonight."

He glances at my shoes and purse on the floor. "You haven't been drinking again, right?"

I sigh and look at the ceiling. I think about saying, <u>Yes, but don't worry. I've got my membership to AA all lined up.</u> Instead, I say, "No."

He comes in and shuts the door. I watch him as he comes around and sits on the couch. He looks perfectly serious. So do I.

"Are you going to tell me what last night was about?"

I look back to the ceiling and sigh. I barely remember last night. "What do you mean?"

"You know what I mean. Why'd you drink so much?"

I shrug. "People do it."

"You don't."

"Yeah, well, there's a first for everything." Lucky me.

"Sam," he says softly, pulling my gaze to him. Our eyes meet and it makes my heart give in, in spite of myself. "Come on, honey," he says gently. "Tell me what's bothering you."

Here it is again. The heartbreak. This time, it feels like a little ball of concentrated pain, squeezing my heart and throat and making it hard to swallow. Who knew heartbreak came in so many different varieties? As I look at Jack's face, his genuine concern for me so evident, a hot tear leaks out and skips down my cheek.

Jack watches it and frowns. "Hey." He scoots to the end of the couch and leans toward me. He's not touching me at all, but I feel wrapped up in him like a cloud. He reaches out and wipes the tear away with his thumb. His touch hums through my body, from cheek to feet.

"If I didn't know better," he says, giving me a gentle, teasing prod on the shoulder, "I'd think you were crying over some guy."

My eyes widen and my reaction comes through on my face before I can stop it. He straightens sharply, blinking in shock.

Great. Just great.

I roll onto my side, away from him, one arm dangling off the table, my face on the edge. Yeah. We just need to stop talking now and he needs to stop looking at me and I need to stop looking at him.

He's quiet so long, I wonder if he's going to leave. Part of me wants him to. Part of me needs him to stay. Because being in love is a special kind of fucked up, I'm discovering.

I close my eyes. Why did he have to come now? Why did I have to fall in love with him?

I hear him get off the couch and walk around the table. It sounds like he's sitting down right in front of me. When I open my eyes, he's lying on the floor on his back, his body parallel to mine. His head is under mine, so I'm looking right at him.

There's no escaping him now.

He's wearing a pained expression I can't interpret. "I'm sorry for teasing you," he says. "Heartbreak sucks."

Hot tears make another appearance, dammit. He reaches up and wipes a tear from my cheek.

I give up.

My heart is aching. He's killing me. I grab his hand, hanging onto it as he cups my cheek and neck.

"Ah, Sammy," he says. "I know this is new for you, but it gets better." He pauses. Again, that expression I can't read. "Usually."

I look at him helplessly. As much as I need and cherish his friendship, how can that ever be enough for me now? How can I pretend?

I tell myself I need to let go of his hand. But when I loosen my grip, instead of taking my hand away the way I meant to, I slide it down to his forearm and grip again, hanging on to Jack for dear life.

He follows the movement of my hand and his brows furrow slightly. He looks back to me, a question in his eyes. I'm too worn out and heartbroken to do anything but look back.

The furrow in his brows deepen. "Who," he asks slowly, "is this guy?"

I press my lips together, the tears running fresh again. I can't look away from him. I can't hide it. Maybe this is what Ashley knew, and why she said to talk to him about it. I can't hide this from him anyway.

A pained look crosses his face: confusion and disbelief. "Sam?" He chokes out my name, his voice a whisper.

It's you. It's you.

And I'm just one more woman he didn't mean to make fall in love with him.

I give a weak shrug and find my voice at last. "Sorry," I whisper. I didn't mean to fall in love with Jack. I really didn't.

His eyes widen slightly in surprise and dawning realization. Now he knows the truth, surely.

It's only inevitable now: his "we'll always be friends" speech, or "I didn't mean to give you the wrong idea" speech, or "I'm in love with Emily" speech. Part of me is cringing against the horrible words I know are coming. Part of me is willing to beg. <u>Beg.</u>

Part of me doesn't want to go one second past this moment, because there's not one single thing Jack can do that won't terrify me.

He has that deer-caught-in-headlights look. He's still processing what I've revealed and he has no idea what to do next. No good can come from this. Why did I have to put the both of us in this awkward fucking position?

This time, I do move, only half an inch, intending to get off the table and away, but his grip on me suddenly tightens, keeping me here.

He's looking at me differently now. Am I just imagining it? Am I reading too much into an expression like those ridiculous love-sick girls are so prone to do? There's no denying I'm officially a ridiculous love-sick girl myself. But he's looking at me almost the way he has in my dreams, like he wants me, too. But it's even more than that. He looks hungry for me. I thought I knew every way

Jack's face could look, but I never could have imagined him looking at me like this.

My heart's pounding against the table and every inch of my skin is on alert. There's that string again, drawing me in whether I want it to or not.

My breathing is sharp and shallow. I now realize, so is his. <u>Oh my God.</u>

He looks like he wants to come to me and I want him too. I'm beyond terrified, but God help me, I want him to so badly.

Still holding my cheek, eyes locked on mine, he lifts his head an inch toward me. I match his move. I didn't mean to. We both freeze.

He's not moving or hardly breathing but he's reeling me in and I'm sunk. I can't fight this.

I lean down half an inch more, asking. Begging. If he pulls back I know it will tear my heart open, but what's the difference? I'm already bleeding.

But he doesn't pull away. He swoops up, coming to me until our lips press together. My heart does, in fact, break open. I am broken everywhere and completely lost in him.

Jack. Jack.

It's just a kiss, but it consumes me. I smell him. His jagged breathing matches mine. My lips are on his, but even though a kiss is what I wanted, it is instantly not enough. I part my lips slightly, needing to taste him. He pulls away, just enough to look at me. He may as well have pulled my heart out of my chest.

I'm terrified I'll see regret in his eyes. Or the look of a friend who's only kissed me out of pity.

Instead I see that look of longing. I've seen it a hundred times on the faces of a hundred different men. It feels so different coming from Jack.

He takes my face into both hands then and kisses me firmly, pressing hard against my mouth. A whimper escapes me. I tighten my grip on his arm, kissing him hard back. Our mouths open eagerly, our tongues desperately tasting each other.

Oh god, oh my god.

He suddenly hooks his arm around my back and slides me off the table on top of him. Our mouths and tongues work together with a kind of desperation I've never experienced. Our arms close around each other like a vise. I'm lightheaded. My heart feels ready to burst, unable to hold this thing in me that is so big and terrible and divine. <u>Oh god.</u> I give a little whimper, completely against my will. Then another.

He moans and grips the back of my head with his hand, pulling me even harder against his mouth. My heart is pounding fiercely and I'm literally dizzy. He rolls us over so he's pressed on top of me and I'm so drunk with him I can only hang on.

Our kissing grows more impassioned and my hands are all over him. All I know are his kisses and his body and everything in me reaching for him.

I can't get him close enough to me. I want him inside me. I mean, I want his entire body inside my entire body and I never knew it was possible to want such a thing. To want a person this way. To want <u>him.</u> All of him. <u>Jack</u>.

I feel his desire for me hard against my inner thigh. My body responds instantly.

Suddenly I'm on fire everywhere, my core aching for him. This is more familiar territory, to be sure, and I feel slightly more sure-footed for a brief moment.

Then that moment goes up in flames.

Even wanting him sexually is different from anything I've experienced before. I can't stop running my hands over his back, feeling the firm muscles under his lightweight t-shirt. But I'm more than touching him, and he's more than touching me. He's tearing through me. Jack is a tsunami of sensation that lights up my skin and sets a blaze deep inside me, reaching deeper into my soul than anyone's ever done before. Even him.

I want him inside me. I <u>need</u> him inside me. He presses himself against me and I wrap my legs around him, angling my hips to press back. The hard length under his jeans grinds into me. His tongue dives deeper as he holds my face like he can't kiss me hard enough. And I can't either. I need him so much.

I run my hand under his shirt onto bare skin. Touching his skin lights me up even more. Suddenly I'm afraid to push it any further. I'm afraid it's all a dream, and that if I'm not careful the magic bubble will pop and it'll be over. He'll change his mind. It'll all stop. As I wrap myself around him and our tongues dive frantically into each other, I'm almost panicked, trying to push down that fear that Jack will suddenly leave me and I won't know how to make him stay.

He abruptly lifts off and away.

"Jack!" I gasp, reaching for him. He was only lifting up so he could remove his shirt. He already had it half way up his chest when he froze, startled by my cry for him.

I've revealed myself yet again. He sees my fear and longing for him and there is no hiding.

It seems to fuel something in him. He looks as hungry for me as I am for him. My breasts are heaving as he tears off his shirt. I've seen his chest a million times. It's almost as familiar to me as his face. But this is different. Everything's different. It's Jack, but more.

He grabs the waistband of my pants. I immediately raise my hips, and he tears my sweats and panties off in one, hurried motion.

His hardness is straining against his jeans. He unbuttons his fly and releases his cock in a flash and I wonder how in the fuck I've never known until now how well-endowed he is.

The only reaction I have is to exhale sharply, because there's no time for anything else. He pushes his jeans to his knees but doesn't take the time to get up and take them off all the way. He gives me a look that tells me I'm about to discover just what Jack can do with that cock and then he's on me again, pushing his mouth hard against me. I'm matching his every move, frantic for him.

His tip finds my entrance like a heat-seeking missile, and he takes me hard and fast. Jack fills me, stretching me and turning that blaze inside me into an inferno. Just when I thought this was already more than a person could take.

We moan together and he rides me hard, my entire body rocking with him.

Oh my god, oh god.

I'm panting, overcome. I didn't know... I didn't know it could be like this. Every inch he moves inside me stirs me up higher and higher. I'm clinging to his bare back, his muscles hard and flexing beneath my arms. He urgently squeezes one breast through my cami, then frantically lifts up the fabric to expose my chest and squeezes it again. He's sucking on my neck and shoulder and jaw. My mouth is working soundlessly with pleasure and shock and desire and wonder. Holy god. My heart is helpless against this.

We kick into a higher gear. More intense. More desperate. More frantic as he works me faster and my body opens to him like I've never opened to anyone. I think I'm going to come undone. He groans low and long in my ear. He almost sounds in pain. I'm panting and whimpering as ecstasy spikes in my body.

Oh god. Omigod.

"Jack," I breathe, biting it out and throwing my head back. He tucks into me, holding his head against my neck as I continue to arch back. Tsunami Jack crashes against me, and I come hard. It's almost frightening. I can't breathe. I can't think. It's the most intense pleasure I've ever felt, tearing through me in one massive wave after another, and then Jack is thrusting helplessly as he empties into me.

The sound he makes only makes my heart yearn for him more.

God, darling.

Through it all, I'm still clinging to him, convulsing and wanting him more than I knew a person could want anyone.

And then we're released. Dropped, more like. The churning storm inside me folds in on itself and recedes, leaving me stunned.

Slick with sweat, our bodies slow. Then become still. Our vise-like holds on one another soften slightly. Except for our labored breathing, we aren't moving at all.

By all my normal standards, what we just did could be called tame. No foreplay. No sexy lingerie. No changing positions. No slapping. No dirty talk. All Jack did was take me in the missionary position and rock me to the fucking core.

And at the same time, I have no idea what this was for him. Was it just a spur-of-the-moment thing? That moment of passion I've always heard can happen between two friends even when it doesn't mean anything? Or was it—

Then I remember. With Jack still in my arms, and still in me and all around me... that's when I remember.

I pinch my eyes closed.

Oh god.

I'm barely breathing now. I don't even need to look at him to know he's remembered, too. I feel it in his body and know it by the way he's suddenly holding his breath. Lord, what have we done?

He slowly, so slowly lifts off me. He doesn't look at me. I can't breathe. I look at his profile and that's when my heart breaks again. Here's another expression I've never seen on him, dripping with pain and guilt and regret. Fuck.

He slowly crawls backwards, sliding out of me and leaving me feeling empty, still not looking at me. As he pulls away and goes to his knees, I pull my top down and draw my legs together. I can't take my eyes off his face.

He slowly hitches up his pants, fastens the button, and pulls up the zipper. He pinches his eyes shut and brings his hands to his face, rubbing them hard over his forehead and into his hair where he grips huge handfuls.

I want to comfort him, but what in the hell do I say?

My wits slowly start coming back to me. We didn't even use a condom. I didn't even think about it. We've talked about this kind of thing before and I know Jack <u>always</u> uses a condom. I always insist on it too, even though I'm on birth control.

What. The fuck. Were we thinking?

But that's not the worst part. Not by a mile. Jack is not over there regretting the lack of a condom. I can only imagine how horrible he's feeling, because I practically feel like <u>I</u> cheated on her. In a way, I did. I knew he was off limits. He's hers, not mine.

I forgot. I forgot he doesn't belong to me.

He gets heavily to his feet and I pull up into a sit, bare legs tucked together to the side, reaching for my sweats. He turns away and I fumble them on, getting into a weak stand myself. My skin still remembers the feel of Jack's touch, but it's slipping away from me. I'm cold and my legs start to shiver.

He grabs his shirt from the floor and works it over his body. Then he looks... lost. He paces to the couch.

"I'm sorry," I say, and I am. No matter what happens next, Jack's the bad guy and someone's heart is broken.

He looks at me then. Our eyes meet, and as so often happens, we're joined together in understanding. I look away. I've seen before how men look at the woman they've strayed with, after they regret it. I don't want to see Jack looking at me that way.

Forget someone's heart being broken. All kinds of hearts will be broken.

He slowly comes back around the table, dully pulls me into his arms against his chest, and holds me there. I circle my arms around his waist, even though I'm afraid I know what this is. I feel the tears welling up but I force them down. I don't want to cry again. I can do that after. Right now I try to hold on to every detail so I can keep them in my mind later: how his arms are wrapped around me, how I'm nestled inside of him, the way his back feels so firm and warm against my hands, the smell of the man I know so well, and the tender way he's holding me, even if it is darkened with regret.

I'm still in my bare feet, but Jack's dressed and even has his shoes on. "I have to go," he says quietly.

I nod against his chest.

Then he plants a gentle kiss on top of my head, pulls away, and leaves without a word, the door clicking softly behind him.

Chapter 15

Jack

I don't think I've ever hated myself more than I do in this moment.

Chapter 16

Sam

I don't call the girls. I don't talk to a soul. I pick up my phone a hundred times to text Jack, but I never do because I don't know what to say.

He doesn't text me either.

I wonder why we don't have memorials for this kind of thing. Because losing Jack feels like a death.

I spend the next few days at work avoiding people as much as I can so I don't have to keep saying "Nothing" when people ask me "What's wrong?" Ashley and Isabella dropped in once, but they didn't stay long.

I'm inconsolable. They don't know what happened, so they think I'm just heartbroken over Jack.

They're not wrong.

For the record, I've been right this entire time: <u>love</u> <u>sucks</u>.

I stay late at the office because I don't want to be home but I don't know what else to do. I've been working so much and am so ahead of schedule on my projects, I'm going to be screwed by the middle of next week when I'm just fucking sitting around twiddling my thumbs.

I don't care.

The girls are busy this evening with one of our group texts. Chloe mentions she hasn't heard from Jack in a while and he's not returning her messages. She has some sort of website question for him. The other girls say they don't know what he's up to either, but this is really nothing new. He doesn't chat with them every day like he used to do with me. So they do what they always do when they want to know what Jack's up to. They ask me.

I don't answer, trusting the conversation will move on to something else, which it does. Ashley says something about a neighbor bringing over a huge box of peaches from their tree, so she's going to divvy it up and bring some round to each of us. I don't reply to that or anything else. I focus on the logo I'm designing instead. It's the only thing I can do that kind of, sort of deadens the pain.

I don't know how I'm going to do it, but I expect I'll spend weeks, months, years, trying to grieve over Jack.

What I don't expect is coming home from work to see his truck parked out front.

I stop right in the middle of the road. He's not in his truck, which means he's in my house. I'm gripping the wheel with both hands, staring at his truck, listening to my car idle in the middle of the empty street.

I take a deep breath, then slowly pull into the drive. When I go through the front door, the living room is empty and the house is quiet.

I shut the door behind me. "Jack?"

194

He comes into view from the kitchen, stopping in the doorway. He's got a half-eaten sandwich in his hand. No plate. Dripping crumbs on my floor.

He looks at me and I can only look back. He looks like hell. Handsome and making my heart ache, but beat to hell.

He glances at the sandwich. "Sorry," he says soberly. "I've been here awhile. I got hungry."

I'm still standing by the door. "It's okay."

"I thought maybe... you saw my truck and didn't want to come in."

Yeah. Kind of. "I had to work late."

"Ah." He looks a little relieved, but still sober. "Want me to make you one?" He lifts the sandwich slightly in question.

What are you doing here, Jack?

"Um..." I say, in response to his question. I don't ever seem to be hungry these days, but I have a headache from the lack of food so I should probably eat. I shrug. "Okay."

He disappears back inside the kitchen. I stand there for a moment, listening to him open and shut the cupboard door, set a plate on the counter, open the fridge.

I slowly walk into the kitchen. He's at the island, the makings of a sandwich laid out before him. I watch him spread mayonnaise on a piece of bread. There's something he wants to say, but I have no idea what and he's clearly not ready to say it yet. I don't know what to say either. I just want to undo all of it and get my friend back.

I quietly set my purse on the counter, followed by my keys. As I take a seat at the bar, I'm watching his every move. As he spreads mustard on the other piece of bread—just how I like it—I watch his hands, his arms. I look at his chest and face. I ache.

He adds ham, tomato, and Swiss cheese, then places the finished product in front of me.

"Thanks." It's the last thing we say for quite some time. I eat my sandwich and he finishes his and we don't say a word. We exchange a few brief glances. I can't read any of them.

Everything's kind of broken down between us and I don't know what to do.

By the time I'm done eating, he's put everything away, wiped down the counter,

196

and loaded the dishes in the dishwasher, including my plate.

Only then does he lean back against the counter and look at me for longer than two seconds. My heart starts in with the goddamned longing again. Why is he here? Why did he have to come here and be live and in person right in my kitchen? He's undoing all the work I've been trying to do to forget him and when he leaves I'll have to start all over again.

Not that I'd gotten very far.

He finally opens his mouth to speak

"I..." He hesitates and I'm all of a sudden very afraid to hear what he's going to say. "I..."

What, Jack? What?

He straightens and frowns and breaks eye contact. "I think there's a game on."

I blink in surprise, then watch as he retreats into the living room, out of my line of sight once more. I hear him sit on the couch and turn on the TV.

I walk across the kitchen toward the living room, my work heels clicking on the tiles. I enter the living room. There he is, right in the middle of the couch, staring at the TV. I look to see who's playing only to find I don't care.

I'm really too exhausted for any of this. If Jack wants to sit on my couch and watch TV, at this exact moment I just don't care.

I slip out of my heels, bend down and pick them up with one hand, and pad down the hall to my bedroom.

I toss my shoes in the closet where they land with an unceremonious thud. I remove my silky neck scarf and hang it on its hook next to the others. I remove my earrings and slide out the drawer to my jewelry tower, tossing the little silver baubles in their place as well.

Jack is in my living room. On my couch.

Maybe I'll just stay here.

I realize I've been staring at the open drawer. I slide it shut. When I turn, Jack's right there in the doorway, watching me.

I startle, putting my hand over my heart. "God, Jack."

"Sorry."

This time, when he looks at me and our gaze holds, I get that feeling I'm used to getting, the feeling I know and understand him.

"Oh, honey," I say sadly.

"I told Emily."

I nod in understanding. "Yeah. I knew you would."

"I... told her that I'm... really sorry."

My heart starts thumping painfully in my chest, little butterflies of panic banging against its walls. "Are you going to try to work things out?"

He furrows his brows at me, seemingly surprised by my question. "No."

The panicked butterflies start to settle down but I'm still afraid of something. I don't even know what.

"I probably wasn't straight with you about how I was feeling about Emily," he says. "It wasn't... I shouldn't have been with her to start with."

<u>Why not?</u> I want to ask, but he goes on.

"Anyway, she's not the kind of woman to put up with that shit."

<u>Good for her,</u> I think. It's what he would've said too, if the situation were different.

"And—" His expression grows more pained, and he's looking at me differently now. Our eyes lock. I don't know if it's desire I see in him, or if I'm just wanting to see that. Whatever it is, it's all mixed up with regret. That I can see plain as day. "Look, I... I really hate that I did that..." My heart clenches in sympathy. Then he starts to come toward me, slowly, one step at a time. My body goes on alert. My heart starts to pump harder.

He's shaking his head, coming closer. "But I'm not as sorry as I know I should be."

There's the string. Pulling, pulling, pulling.

Wait. I'm standing my ground. Or trying to. I don't know what this is.

"It was the worst thing I've ever done to anyone." Closer, closer. Larger than life. I'm stuck to the floor. "It was so stupid." He's right in front of me now.

We're not touching at all, but somehow, I feel him anyway. I can't look away from his eyes.

"And it was just... selfish," he continues, tightly. "All I was thinking about was how much I wanted you. Even the way I took you—" I feel a rush of heat, remembering exactly how he took me, "—even that was selfish because I wasn't making sure you were..." he pauses for the briefest moment, then spits it out, "you know, getting there or thinking about protection or thinking about anything."

"Me either," I whisper.

He puts his hands on my upper arms and that's it. My body starts to purr. Oh lord.

"All I could think about was how much I needed you. I needed you so much."

I don't know exactly if he means need me the way guys need girls, their bodies taking over everything, or needs me the way I need him. Because even though I'm not supposed to, I do need him. I need him more than I've ever needed anyone, and as we hover here, looking at one another, I think he has to know it.

"I still need you," he says quietly.

His mouth slowly dips down toward mine. I am once again helpless to resist. I thoughtlessly go up on tiptoe to meet him. When his lips press gently against mine, I'm wishing I were lying down again, because I'm nearly knocked over. I bring my hands to his sides, hanging on.

His hands travel from my arms to my back, never leaving my body. He gently pulls me to him and I go where he wants me to go. I am his to control. Our bodies press together, chest to hip to knee. I lean against him, knees softening, and he holds me tighter.

He pulls away just enough to look at me with those blue eyes of his. God, Jack.

I should ask him what he's thinking and what this means but I don't want to talk. I want Jack to kiss me. I want him to take me. I need him to. I slowly slide my hands under the hem of his shirt, softly touching his skin. My blood is coursing through my body. I look at him tentatively, asking.

There's a half second pause, then he bends his knees slightly and lifts me off my feet. My heart swoops and I let out a little gasp, reflexively wrapping my legs around his chest. As many times as Jack's picked me up, it's never been like this. Already he's

202

sweeping me downstream again. Tsunami Jack.

He gives me that heated look and I try to keep my wits about myself. I lean in to kiss him and that's when I know it's a good thing he's holding me. No way could I stand on my own two feet. I'm tumbling away, right here in Jack's arms.

His arms tighten around me as we open to each other. Not like the hard, desperate kisses from before, this is a softer, exploring kiss. It still takes me from hot to blazing in a matter of moments. He turns and carries me toward the bed and I respond by holding him tighter, indicating my approval of this plan.

When we reach the bed, he sets me on the mattress on my knees, facing him. He's standing in front of me. Panting, we lift the hem of each other's shirts at the same time. I remove his first, then lift my arms so he can remove mine. His eyes sweep over me, then he cups me with both hands, over the black lace of my bra. I let out a shaky exhalation. Everything he does to me is like lightning.

I put my hands on his bare chest. His skin is hot to the touch. Keeping one hand on my breast, he reaches around and unhooks my bra quicker than I can do it. The straps slide off my shoulders and the material slips off. He exhales in appreciation, glancing at my face as he tosses the bra aside, then dips down and takes me into his mouth. I gasp and grab the hair on the back of his head. I'm gripping his shoulder with my other hand and he still has me in one arm, pulling me in closer by my lower back.

Even on my knees, I'm sinking. My breaths are short and ragged. I'm soaked and ready for him. His strong arm supports me as he sucks and caresses my breast, working me into a frenzy before swinging over and sucking on the other side. I'm gripping his shoulder hard, my chin tucked down so I can watch his tongue sliding over and encircling my hard nipple. He takes me into his mouth and gives me a long, lingering suck, pulling my breast outward slightly, before letting go and circling my nipple with his tongue again.

"God, Jack," I breathe.

Still attached to my breast he looks up at me. Then he pulls me down slightly by the back of the neck, and makes short work of moving from my nipple to my mouth. Jack's tongue works expertly with mine. His hand slides up the outside of my thigh, under my skirt, and to my ass, where he squeezes me hard. He slips his fingers under the lacy elastic of my panties, running his fingertips along my soft folds. I hitch my knees farther apart. I'm suddenly dying to find out what else Jack can do with his tongue.

As if reading my mind, he picks me up again and throws my legs around his waist so he can lay me on my back. He's lowering his face between my legs, which I'm opening wider—<u>for Jack!</u> He doesn't bother removing my panties. He hooks two fingers around the material of the crotch, yanks it to one side, and dives his tongue into me. <u>Holy god.</u> My legs spread further and my head arches back in one, joint movement. Jack's tongue is all over me, licking and sucking and teasing and circling. One hand is gripping my side, just above my hip, and I'm gripping his arm.

I'm exhaling sharply, over and over, curling inward and bringing my legs higher. He stops for a second so he can yank my panties off. I'm aching for him every half second I'm without his touch, but it isn't long. He dives back, this time also teasing my opening with the tip of one finger. He circles my clit with his tongue, and slowly penetrates me, gently moving that finger in a circle too, so he's pressing all around the side of my walls.

Fuck.

"More," I gasp. "More." And he does slide into me more, then more. So deep. Then again, with two fingers. "More." Then again, slowly, with three. Then harder and faster.

Oh god.

My legs tremble as Jack fucks me. I want to cry out, but I'm literally afraid I'm losing my mind, so I bite down my cry. Tongue circling and sucking my clit, fingers pumping me fast, Jack draws me higher and higher. With his free hand, he rubs the hot skin on my stomach and squeezes my breast. I squeeze the other one myself as every part of me that can arch, is arching. Neck, back, hips, legs, I'm straining open and trembling as Jack takes me right over the edge.

Lights burst behind my closed eyes as I climax against him. He doesn't slow and that only makes me come harder, and draws it out longer. I'm still trying to bite back what would be a scream and manage just to whimper instead, over and over again. My body is thrashing helplessly. I don't think I've ever, ever felt anything like this.

It takes a moment, but I finally come down in powerful, crashing waves, until I'm left limp and panting on the bed. I weakly look down at Jack, my mouth parted slightly. He gives me a satisfied half-grin. I have a feeling that man knows exactly what he just did to me. All I can do is gape back at him and try not to be a puddle.

He wipes his mouth and stands, looking down at me. His chest muscles flex as he undoes his pants and brings out a raging erection.

He whips out his wallet and extracts a shiny, foil packet before tossing his wallet on the floor. I shock myself, because I want to tell him not to bother. I bite my bottom lip instead. He rolls the condom on and, once again, I'm wondering where in the hell he's been hiding that massive specimen of manhood he's got. He strips the rest of the way then, pulling my skirt off too. He crawls up the bed to me, both of us fully nude.

I never realized before what a vulnerable thing that is.

But then Jack looks at me and tucks me into an embrace and I feel safe in his presence. Except for the tsunami part. Because as soon as he slides into me, oh so slowly, I'm carried away again. I'm all ablaze, again. I'm clinging to him desperately and he's rocking me with more and more passion, again.

His body is weighing heavily on my stomach and chest. He's filling me completely, hitting my spot perfectly. All I can do is rock my hips in answer and hungrily taste his neck and shoulders and hang on for the ride. I feel like I should be showing him I actually have some moves, but Jack's rendered me helpless. And in some ways, this is all I want. Him, inside me, holding me, sweeping me downstream even though it terrifies me.

He hooks one arm under my knee and brings me up higher, giving us even more friction.

I'm gasping again. I press my forehead against his shoulder, my core getting hotter and hotter as he makes me climb again.

"Do you like that, sweetheart?" he says thickly.

My heart swoops at the sound of his voice. I nod urgently against him, whimpering because I'm climbing even higher.

"I loved eating you out," he says, the pleasure in my body spiking hard just at the sound of his voice. "You tasted so good, Sam."

"Oh god," I bite out, because I'm getting ready to come. "Fuck, Jack."

"Damn right."

My climax takes me hard, thrashing me helplessly as Jack continues to ride me. I clutch his back and bite his shoulder. Again and again, waves of pleasure crash through my body and I'm whimpering and panting helplessly. <u>Oh fuck.</u>

Jack's getting harder and pumping me faster. The grips of my orgasm start their first release and I gasp for breath. Then Jack releases too. His shuddering movements push me back up into a fresh wave and I contract hard around him.

We ride the waves out together, his rhythms slowing. Soon, he's going so slow, he's almost caressing me with his still-firm cock. Just to make the devastation of the tsunami complete, he gives me a deep, lingering kiss that reaches all the way to the bottom of my soul.

When he finally pulls away, we're softly panting, and looking one another in the eye. He's not moving, not doing anything to my body really, but I'm falling deep into those striking blue eyes. It goes on and on, what Jack can do to me.

I tuck my forehead into his neck. His embrace around me tightens. I grip him harder too.

"You're amazing, Sam."

<u>I didn't even do anything</u>. But I look up at him anyway, and let him kiss me again. It's so sweet and so tender, I melt right into the mattress, but I somehow gather enough strength to kiss him back.

Chapter 17

Sam

We're lying in bed on our sides, facing one another. We're still nude, but the covers are draped loosely over our waists. His arm is under my head and I'm resting my hand on his bicep. His other hand is resting on the mattress, his fingers lightly caressing my stomach. Our calves are intertwined gently.

I'm feeling a little wobbly on the inside, after everything that's happened. I think he is too, because as we talk, we're struggling a bit to find our feet.

Maybe it's because there are things we're not saying. At least, there are things I'm not saying. Because I can't stop thinking about what he's doing to me, how overpowering it is to be with him. It's a little easier in this moment, because I'm not trying to consume him, all while he's consuming the hell out of me. But even just lying here he's this powerful presence, and I feel on the edge of something bigger than me.

How do I tell Jack those things?

Then there's the other thing. The terrible thing we did. I want to know how he feels about that. I want to know what he's been going through since then and how he feels now. But I don't know if he wants to talk about it yet. Or ever.

Then there are all the things I'm flat afraid to ask about. I don't understand what Emily was to him. I don't know what I am to him, now that we've crossed this line. I really don't know what we're doing.

And I don't know how to start talking about any of it.

It doesn't help that I see something weighing on him.

So I give voice to the one thing in my heart I feel I can say aloud. "I missed you, Jack."

His face softens. "Did you?"

"Of course," I say softly. "Dork."

There's a brief smile. "I missed you, too." Then, he's back to looking heavy.

My fingers absently caress his bicep. He's taken to watching his own fingers, as they trace lightly on my stomach and my scar, sending ripples of sensation all over me.

"Do you..." he pauses and I search his face. He's not looking at me on purpose. I have a feeling that whatever he's getting ready to say, it's the thing he's needed to say since he got here. It's the thing he couldn't say in the kitchen, and it's something that's been lingering with him. "Do you see me differently now?"

He glances at me hesitantly, but I don't get his meaning.

"Because of before," he clarifies.

Ah. "The fallen man," I say, understanding now, but his face falls and I instantly regret it.

"I really, really wish I could go back and do things differently," he says. "Not... being with you. That I'd keep." I feel a warm flush slide over my body. "But I wish I could go back and not be with her. I should've broken up with her before. It wasn't fair to her and

214

she didn't deserve to be with someone who wasn't really with her. And she <u>really </u>didn't deserve... you know."

This is eating him up. I knew it would.

"And now... now I'm always going to be that guy."

I sigh. There's no easy fix to this, but I can't stand that he's re-writing who he thinks he is. "Jack—"

"Don't try to tell me it wasn't a big deal," he says firmly.

"I wasn't going to," I say, just as firmly. "It was stupid. Awful. I wish I could take it back, too."

"You didn't do anything wrong," he says, frowning.

"Yes, I did." He looks ready to argue with me, but I hold up my hand to stop him. "Hey, you feel bad, and I feel bad, because it was bad. It was." I lower my hand, resting it on his chest now. "And you're never going to look back on that and think it was okay. We fucked up."

"I fucked up."

I sigh. "I can see you're determined to beat yourself up over it. Well, that's fine.

Maybe you need to do that for a while. But at some point you're going to have to let it be in your past. You're going to have to move on. And you're going to have to allow yourself to understand that <u>one</u> moment, even a moment like that, doesn't necessarily change everything else about you."

"I really hate that I did that."

"I know, sweetheart. I hate it, too."

"I feel like...." He brings his fingertips up to my cheek, and watches as he strokes it. "Like I don't deserve to be happy now."

His eyes meet mine, and even in the middle of a conversation like this, there's that swept away feeling again. I swear to God, I really don't know if I can handle this. I feel like if I don't hang on to something with both hands, it's going to tear me to shreds. But I don't know what the fuck to hang on to.

But there's one thing I know, and that's this: if anyone deserves to be happy, it's Jack.

"You can be happy," I say. "It's okay. I promise. It doesn't make you a horrible person. Emily's going to go on and live her life and do all kinds of things and have happiness and sorrow that has nothing to do with you. Her life doesn't revolve around you now. She's just... going to go on and live her life because that's what people do. That's what you have to do, too."

"But..." His hand stills, warm and soft on my cheek. There's so much pain in his voice and on his face. My heart just breaks. "Do you see me differently now?"

I shake my head slowly. I do see him differently now, but not for the reason he thinks. "No, sweetie. I don't see you differently."

"You promise?"

Jack, stop this. I bring my hand to his cheek and caress him gently. His eyes lock on mine, hurting and desperate. "I promise." He blinks at me, his expression unchanged.

I slowly scoot closer to him and hold his face in my hand. I give him a gentle kiss. "I promise," I whisper.

His expression starts to soften. He's giving way, but not there yet. I kiss him again, and this time I linger. I put every ounce of love I feel for this man into that kiss. My own tenderness surprises me. I didn't know I had it in me. I swear, I didn't.

I pull away, and there's what I wanted to see. He believes me now. "I promise," I say again, holding his eyes.

His arms come around me, one hand on the back of my head. He brings me to him for a kiss, and this time, he's the one in control. He kisses me firmly, deeply and I kiss him back. He overpowers me. It's crazy how quickly it happens.

Still kissing me, he rolls me onto my back, his weight on top of me. His hardness is gentle and firm against my thigh. He's gentle and firm on me everywhere. He pulls away and looks at me, his hand stroking my cheek. "I do want to be happy," he says. "I want to be happy with you, Sam."

My heart's pounding out of my chest. I'm scared, I want to say, but he's pulling, pulling, pulling and I'm going right along.

"Is that all right?" he asks quietly, those brilliant blue eyes holding me.

I give a slight nod, terrified, then kiss him. Because even though he terrifies me, there's so much comfort in him, too.

Chapter 18

Jack

The next morning, in the shadowy light of pre-dawn, I wake for a few seconds, aware of only two things. One, I'm happy. I'm indescribably, unworthily, helplessly, sky-over-the-moon happy. Two, Sam is readjusting herself back into my arms. She's still asleep, from what I can tell. She'd been on her side, facing away from me, my arm around her. Now she's snuggling back into me, tucking her head onto my shoulder, and letting out a long breath as she settles in.

We're now in almost the same position we were in when we fell asleep in last night. It strikes me that over the course of the night, she hasn't gone far. She hasn't been throwing her arms and legs all over the place, tossing and turning like she usually does.

This woman always sleeps like there's something a bit restless inside of her. But not now.

No.

Sam is in my arms, nestled into me, one arm around my side. Her breathing is soft and calm. Her presence washes clean over me and my heart swells right out of my chest. I close my eyes and settle in deeper, drawing my arms more snugly around her warm, naked body. I fall back asleep with a smile on my face.

I'm destined to wake with a smile on my face, too, thanks to Sam. This time—it must be an hour or so later based on the light in the room—Sam's sitting up and straddling my thighs. She's running her hands down my chest, then slowly lower to my stomach, then slowly lower to my...

"Ho there," I say sleepily, my eyebrows raising.

She grins at me and my heart starts pumping. My cock's already pumping. She gives me a devious look.

"What are you up to, missy?" I'm waking rapidly.

"The question is, what are <u>you</u> up to?" She's already got the base of my cock in one hand, and is shimmying her gorgeous, naked body down my legs so she can lean over my shaft. Well, good <u>morning</u>.

I open my mouth to say something clever, but fuck if I know what it was because she just put her wet mouth over my head and somehow manages to suck on the tip in pulses as she takes me in deeper and deeper.

I drop my head to the pillow and exhale long and deep, rubbing my hand on her shoulder. She comes back up, again doing god-knows-what to make my rod feel like that.

It's not that I'm exactly <u>surprised</u> that Sam knows what to do with the business end of my dick, but good <u>lord.</u>

She cups and squeezes the tip of my cock with one hand, then gently lifts my sack with the other. "I—" Again, thought obliterated as she takes my balls into her warm, wet mouth. I open my legs a bit to give her more room to work. As a thank you, she works me up so well I don't even know where I am. It's only Sam sucking my balls, expertly working my shaft with her hands, licking and sucking my cock, back to taking my balls in her mouth, back to my dick. This woman is perfection.

She's been taking me deep, but when I feel her open up and take me clear into the back of her throat, she damn near makes me shoot my load right then. This is a rare treat, let me tell you, because most girls find my length way too much to handle properly.

"Fuck, Sam."

I look down and watch her gorgeous mouth working my shaft and it's all I can do to keep it together. But her pretty little ass is sticking up in the air and I want it. And I mean now.

"Get up here, woman," I say thickly.

My dick still in her mouth, she manages to look up at me and give me a devious grin. She brings her mouth up to the tip, deposits an extra amount of saliva, and slides back down so slick while sucking me firmly.

My head falls back on the pillow again and I angle my hips slightly toward her mouth. Damn. I know what she wants. She's determined to make me come, but I know what I want too. I want inside her, this minute. I hook my hands under her biceps, pulling her firmly toward me. She grins at me again—man, this girl is so damned sexy—and slowly starts crawling up my body.

"Whatever do you want?" she asks innocently, aiming herself right over my erect cock and wiggling her ass.

"Big tease." She grins, but I need her right now. She knows it, too. "Where the fuck are the condoms?" We cleaned out the supply in my wallet last night.

"Nightstand."

I look over, grateful to see the drawer is within reach. As I pull out the box, she's back to stroking my shaft with both of her hands. I tear open the package and start to put the condom on but she takes over, using one hand after another to roll it all the way down. She's not just putting it on, she's stroking me and squeezing me and threatening to send me into heaven.

My eyes rake over her. I take in her breasts, the curve of her stomach, the pink lips of her sex. Since she's still straddling me, she's hovering right above my thighs. When she's done and starting to climb back up, I grab her hips and bring her into position, slowly inserting myself into her tight warmth. I close my eyes and groan.

"Is that what you wanted?" she asks, starting to ride me slow and glorious.

"Fuck, yes."

I open my eyes so I can watch her watching me. It goes straight to my heart. <u>Damn, girl</u>. I run my hands down her full breasts, her soft stomach, her sweet mound. I watch my cock going in and out of her. I still can't get over how deep she's able to take me. I thrust up to meet her, but she's controlling the rhythm and it's driving me mad. I could come any minute, but I hold out. Ladies first.

I use one finger to tease her little bud. Her eyes flutter shut, and she tightens around my dick. <u>That's right, darlin'.</u>

I bring my finger to my tongue and taste her sweet juices as I deposit a generous dollop of saliva on the tip of my finger. I go back to her clit, slick as I rub her now. She throws her head back, arching her back. She's breathing heavy and losing control. "Damn you, Jack," she whispers, and I grin.

She glances at me, a sexy look of determination in her eyes. Still riding me, she shimmies her knees a little further apart so she can take me even deeper, then she slowly leans backwards until she's resting her hands on the bed behind her. My cock thickens even more, as every ridge of her rubs against me, her breasts in the air.

Fuck. I'm right there on the edge, my breaths coming in ragged spurts. I've never had to fight so hard to control myself like I've had to with her, and here I am again, ready to blow my wad first like an untrained teenager. But she's so damned sexy and feels so incredible and I love her so fucking much she's driving me wild.

I manage to keep it together though, as she rocks on me harder and faster, as I keep one hand strumming her engorged clit, as my other hand roams everywhere I can reach: along her thigh, over her stomach, cupping and squeezing her breasts, rolling her hard nipples between my fingers.

She sits up, her beautiful face flushed and full of ecstasy—I adore that look on her— and comes to me. Her body presses against me and her mouth joins mine. I hold her tight, sliding into her harder and faster now that my hips are unpinned. She whimpers, her chest flushing hot, as I start kissing and suckling her soft neck. I smack her bare ass hard. Again, harder.

She climaxes, gasping and convulsing over me, and I finally let my body go. All the pleasure I've been reigning in rushes in a high, hot peak. Every muscle in my body flexes and I'm delirious with pleasure. She's contracting so hard, it feels like she's sucking on me, determined to milk every last drop.

God, she's perfection. She blows the 1 to 10 scale clear out of the fucking water.

When it's over, we're both on our backs, panting weakly. I'm stunned. Every time, she leaves me stunned. I glance over, giving her a dopey grin. I can't help it. "That's one way to wake me up."

"I had to sneak attack you," she says breathlessly, "before you made me all loopy again."

"Huh?"

"I had to prove I'm not <u>completely</u> useless in bed."

I chuckle, still trying to catch my breath. "Darlin, if the other times were your version of useless, I am one lucky bastard."

It's past time for Sam to start getting ready for work, yet here we still are. I have a meeting with a client this morning, too. I have just enough time to dash home, take a quick shower, and get my tail to the coffee house.

I lean over Sam anyway, drinking in her smell and her kiss and her amazing body. She wraps her legs around my waist and I know I'm sunk. The only question is, do I text my client that I need to reschedule before or after I make Sam mine again? But it's a big client and I really shouldn't.

My hand goes to one of her ample breasts and squeezes. "Jack," she breathes. My cock pulses hot at the sound of her saying my name. "Work," she whispers.

I know she's right. We have to stop. I groan, ducking my head down to the crook of her neck and sucking gently. She tastes so good.

We hear the rattling of a lock and the front door open.

We jolt apart and look at one another for half a second. She scrambles that lovely, naked body out of bed, nearly getting caught up in the covers. I grin at her.

"Sam?" Ashley's voice calls. Sam dashes toward her closet and I climb out of bed, bending down for my clothes. "Jack?" I realize my truck parked out front is a dead giveaway.

"Yo!" I answer. Sam glares at me as she disappears into the closet, but I can only grin back as I step into my briefs.

By the time Ashley makes an appearance at the bedroom door, I've hitched up my jeans. As she was coming down the hall, she was saying, "I put the peaches on the—" but when she sees me she halts, wide-eyed.

"Hey Ashley, babe." I button the top button and zip the zipper.

She blinks at me as I pick up my shirt and pull it on. Sam comes out of the closet wearing her black, silk robe, crossing her arms and leaning against the door jamb and looking flustered. It's cute as hell.

"I have a meeting," I say, approaching Ashley, who's still blinking at me, speechless. "I gotta run." I give her a kiss on the cheek.

"Uh, bye." She glances at Sam.

I turn to Sam, who's gathered some composure and is trying to play it cool. "As for you." I grab her around the waist, snake my other hand into the back of her hair, and plant a kiss full on the mouth.

She makes a little sound of protest and her fists go to my chest, like she's going to push me away. Half a heartbeat later, she softens in my arms and lets me hold her close. God, I love making this woman melt, even though I know it's against her will.

Oh hell, who am I kidding? <u>Especially</u> because it's against her will.

I pull back and she sways a bit. I hold her by her upper arms so she can catch her balance. <u>Score one for the Jack-meister.</u>

When I cast around for my shoes, I notice Ashley gaping at us, her mouth a big "O." My shoes are by the closet—I don't even remember taking them off—so I hop over and pick them up. This gives me a chance to pass Sam on my way out. I give her a grin and a firm slap on the ass. She jumps, then crosses her arms and scowls at me. "See you later, sexy. Bye, Ashley."

Ashley's grinning widely now. "Bye, Jack."

Just before I leave the room, Ashley spins toward Sam, wearing a gleeful expression.

I bound out the front door to discover it's the most beautiful day Central California has ever seen.

Chapter 19

Sam

Ashley's grinning at me like the Cheshire cat just ate the fucking white rabbit. "I knew it."

I groan and drop my head in my hands. After the night I just had, I'm spinning and need a soft place to land. I don't know if I can handle all this <u>glee.</u>

She laughs—<u>laughs</u>—then says, "I know this wasn't part of your life plan, but try not to freak out too badly."

"I'm not freaking out."

"Uh-huh."

"But I do need to get ready for work," I say, scowling. "Don't you have someplace to be?"

"Yeah." But she doesn't move and is still smiling at me.

"For Pete's sake, what?"

"Don't I get any details?"

"You want <u>details?</u> Are you crazy?"

"Well, I don't need you to tell me if he's hung or anything."

"Ashley!"

"Because we already know he is."

"Wait. Say what?" <u>What the hell?</u> "Have you been checking out Jack's package?"

"Uh, it's <u>kinda</u> hard to miss. It's not like you've never noticed either."

I'm shaking my head firmly. I hardly know what to think about having this kind of conversation with Ashley. Isabella, maybe. Chloe, sure. But <u>Ashley?</u>

"I thought we'd all talked about it," she says, in the same tone of voice someone might say, 'Hmm, I wonder what the weather's going to be like tomorrow?'

"You people are <u>talking</u> about it?"

"I thought for sure you were there for that conversation." She gives me an incredulous look. "Wait," she says seriously. "You've really never looked at Jack's package?" She's giving me that weird look again. Like she understands something about

232

me that I don't. "You look at everyone's package. If I had a package, you'd be checking it out."

"You've got a nice rack," I say, hoping to deflect the conversation because I don't think I like where it's going.

She crosses her arms and puts one finger to her mouth, thinking. "That's so weird. It's almost like... something in you knew Jack was the one for you, so you just wouldn't go there in your mind at all."

I blink.

Is that what it was?

Wait, whoa, whoa, whoa. Who said anything about The One?

"Wow," she says. "Jack's broken through a pretty big barrier, hasn't he?"

Never mind. She understands something about me I understand just fine. "Ya think?"

"Are you okay?"

"No, I'm freaking the fuck out."

She's back to laughing again, though it's more gently this time. "It's okay, Sam. You'll be fine. It's still just Jack."

"There's nothing just Jack about it. I just... I don't know what to think. I have no idea what we're doing."

In fact, now that I'm out of his presence and not under his spell, I have so many questions. How long has he felt... however he feels? Just what <u>does</u> he feel for me? There's no denying I've fallen in love with that big freaking dork, like it or not, but is he in love with me or what is this? He says he wants to be happy with me, but what in the hell does that mean?

"Well, what does Jack say?"

"About what?"

"About what you two are doing."

"I don't know. I haven't asked him. I can't talk to him about stuff like this."

"Sam," Ashley says, exasperated, "you talk to Jack about everything. Why should this be different?"

Because, because, because.

I shrug, being the pain in the ass that I am.

"Okay, look. You need to just... relax. Enjoy it, Sam. This is the good stuff."

Is it?

She checks the time on her phone and jolts. "Crap. I actually do have to go. Call me later, okay?"

I nod, but I don't know what to think. If it's not Jack spinning me in circles, it's Ashley.

She comes over and gives me a hug that smells a little too much like glee. Then she gives me a look that's a pretty talented combination of sternness and amusement. "Talk to him. He's still your best friend, you know."

I'm half way through my work day, but I still can't seem to get my head out of my ass. It's a good thing I was ahead on my projects, because this day has been about as productive as napping. My mind is all over the place.

Well, okay, mostly it's just in one place. I keep having the most heat-inducing flashbacks to being with Jack. It's more than a little distracting. Then, I can't help freaking out about the fact that I don't know thing <u>one</u> about any of this. I don't do love. I don't do relationships.

I mean, are Jack and I in a relationship now? Are we supposed to go out for romantic evenings, sit at candle-lit tables, and gaze sloppily into each other's eyes? Even the simplest things are throwing me off when I think about them. For example, I try to imagine him dropping by my house like he always does and I don't even know how I'm supposed to greet him. I'm thinking the whole fist-bump thing might not be appropriate anymore.

As if reading my mind, I get a text from Jack: <u>Pick you up at 6?</u>

My heart lifts just seeing a text from him, but my nerves shoot up too. I take a deep breath. I try to remember what Ashley said. He's still my best friend.

Me: Where are we going?

Jack: It's a surprise.

A surprise? Cue the girly squealing.

Just kidding.

Me: What am I supposed to wear to this surprise? Skirt, jeans, bathing suit?

Jack: Why isn't naked an option?

Okay, joking around is a little better. Even if it is joking about being naked around my best friend.

Me: Who says it's not?

Jack: Nice casual. You in or what?

There are those damned nerves again. At least he's not having me dress up.

Me: Is this a date?

Jack: I sure as hell hope so.

Me: Okay.

Jack: Try not to sound too excited.

Me: Well I had big plans to clip my nails tonight.

Jack: I'll try to get you and your nails back early then.

I smile.

Jack: But no promises.

All I can say is, when Jack picks me up for our "date" I'm glad there are no witnesses around to see it. I'm so nervous about how I'm supposed to act that I watch for his truck through the living room window and am halfway down the sidewalk before he even comes to a stop. I figure if I can just hop in before he gets out, I eliminate the whole hug versus fist-bump problem.

"Hey," I say, climbing in and buckling up. My heart is going a little too fast for my comfort. God, this is weird.

He's giving me an amused look. "Hey, yourself."

"So where are we going?" I'm just going to try to act normal. <u>He's still my best friend. He's still my best friend.</u>

I glance at him as he pulls out, still with that grin on his face. <u>My really hot best friend. Damn, this guy is good-looking.</u> My heart flips over in my chest, which is totally not helping my fucking nerves. He's wearing a nice blue shirt with short-sleeves—so I can see the muscles flexing in his arms as he turns the wheel—and casual slacks, which are sporting a sizeable bulge. Okay, yeah, I can see why the girls have talked about it. It's still a mystery how I managed to not look before, but whatever. This whole situation is confusing the hell out of me, so what's one more thing?

"Do you remember that I set up the new website for Terrace Creek Olive Mill a few months back?" he says, apparently beginning to answer my question.

I nod. "They're the ones on the way to Swan Pointe right? Or was that the brewery?"

"That's them. The brewery's over on South Street."

"Oh, that's right." I'm starting to relax a tiny bit. We're just talking. I can do that.

"Well, Sean, he's the owner, he said he'd give us a private tour."

"Oh, cool."

"Yeah. I've been wanting to check it out."

Okay, I can do that. I don't ask if we're going to dinner afterwards because, you know, the whole romantic love-gazing thing. But a tour's cool. How sappy can a person be on a date when there's a tour guide along? I like the idea of a buffer.

Speaking of buffers, I realize where I'm sitting. Jack's truck has a bench seat, so I could've sat in the middle, right next to him.

It's not where I normally sit, obviously, but it's what I would've done with any other guy. In fact, I could unbuckle and scoot over right now. But I don't.

Instead, as we head out of town and make the twenty minute drive through the foothills and to our destination, I'm just trying to do my part to carry on a conversation. I'm still feeling off-balance though, so Jack's doing most of the heavy lifting. He takes to talking about a job he's working on and I'm glad. I just want to listen.

Eventually we pull into a gravel parking lot next to a charming, mission-style building with red roof tiles. An ornate wooden sign reads: "Terrace Creek Olive Mill. Olive Oil. Goods. Eatery." At first glance, it looks like the building is a store-front with a restaurant attached. The other building is set back a bit and much larger. I assume that's the actual mill.

I'm intrigued and grateful for the distraction of something new, because as Jack kills the engine I get nervous all over again. Here we go. For the first time in a very long time, I wish I were more like other girls so I wouldn't be acting and feeling so weird.

"Stay put." He points a finger at me and gives me a grin. My heart flips over, <u>again,</u> and he gets out of the truck. In another two seconds, I realize he's going to open the door for me. This kind of surprises me, because Jack and I have talked about this particular chivalrous tradition. I'd really rather open my own damned door, to be honest, instead of sitting here like an invalid.

When he opens the door, he says, "I figured I needed a head start so you couldn't run right in there without me."

I scowl at him. "Har har."

He grins and extends his hand. My heartbeat speeds up again and I hesitate for just a moment, but then I take it. This morning, I damn near got myself off sucking this guy's cock, but ask me to hold his hand and I get all shy about things.

Yeah, it doesn't make sense to me either.

"You look nice," he says, as we head toward the building.

That's definitely a date kind of thing to say. I'm wearing slim black pants (I couldn't deal with strutting my stuff in a skirt while on a date with Jack, sorry) and a loose, off-the shoulder top.

"Thanks." But I don't look at him. "You, too."

He kind of chuckles. I want to ask him what's so fucking funny, but I have a feeling I know so I don't say anything.

I take a deep breath. Okay, I need to try to get it together. Like Ashley said, he's still my best friend. The fact that my hand is actually <u>tingling</u> from holding his, well... that's okay, I guess. It's probably good, or something.

Right?

I take another deep breath.

After about four more steps of walking hand in hand, Jack lifts our hands slightly so he can hip-bump me.

"Hey!" I grin at him. Still holding his hand, I bump him back. "Brat."

He lets go of my hand long enough to zing my side. Still grinning, I swat at his hand with both of mine. "Cut it out."

He laughs and takes my hand again. This time, it's nice. He squeezes me and I squeeze him back. "We're going around this way," he says, pointing.

He leads us past the main entrance—I glance through the open doors to see there is, in fact, a little store in there—and around to the side of the building. The restaurant's patio comes into view. There's a couple dozen wrought-iron tables on a herringbone, brick patio, which is shaded by a wooden lattice thick with flowering vines. The whole area has a sweeping view of the olive grove. There are diners dressed kind of nice, like we are, but also some in jeans and capris, so the atmosphere is charming while being casual.

"Smells good." I eye the plates someone's table as we go by. The table's occupants are sharing their appetizers: a caprese salad with a beautiful drizzle of olive oil, and some crostini with olive tapenade. Chloe would love this.

"Want to eat here?" he asks.

"Did you have something else planned?"

"No, I thought this would be fun. The food's supposed to be really good."

"Okay." This is a great idea. There's not even any candles on the tables. I'm warming up to this date more and more all the time.

In fact, things get easier as we go along. After walking right through the employee entrance to find the owner, I'm spared wondering if Jack's going to introduce me as his friend or girlfriend, when Sean extends his hand to me and gives me a friendly, "You must be Sam."

He's a surprisingly young guy, around our age, and pretty fun to talk with. We're given a tour of the facility, including areas they don't typically open for their public tours. He shows us the big vats while he explains how they make all their different oils. I almost forget we're even on a date. By the time we've thanked Sean and are on our own in the store sampling every flavor of olive oil they have—my favorite is the roasted garlic—we're joking and goofing around.

Surprisingly, the store has way more than just their oils for sale. In addition to getting a few bottles of different kinds of oil, we end up getting a jar of stuffed olives, a loaf of fresh sourdough bread, and some macadamia

244

nut turtles they make on site. We haul it all out to Jack's truck so we don't have to fool with it at the restaurant.

"I'm worried that chocolate will melt though," Jack says, as we load in our bags.

"You're full of crap," I say, because I know what he really wants. I open the package and hold it out so he can take one of the turtles.

He grins and takes one and so do I. We bite in at the same time, and at the same time close our eyes and make yummy noises.

"Oh my god," I say. This thing is heaven. Why did we only get four?

Jack nods, but he's too busy eating to talk.

We finish our first ones and go for the remaining two. "We need to get more of these before we leave."

"Hm-hmm," Jack agrees, licking his fingers.

Yes, watching him lick those fingers makes my heart skip a beat. So does the look he's starting to give me.

Oh, yeah, I definitely remember we're on a date now.

Before I know what's happened, he's cupped my face in his hands and is planting a firm kiss on my lips. He smells of Jack and chocolate. Yet again, I'm hanging onto his sides to keep from falling over.

He pulls away with a sultry grin, but I want more. I tug him back so we can do it again. This time, we sink into it. Our mouths open to each other and I get the faint taste of chocolate. He wraps one arm around my waist, and I bring a hand to his firm jaw, then up to the back of his neck. As I run my fingers into his soft hair, he squeezes me tighter. <u>Holy hell.</u>

He brings it to an end just in time, because apparently there's just so much Jack I can handle without getting overwhelmed. We walk back towards the building, fingers laced together, and my legs just the tiniest bit unsteady. But I'm trying to hang on.

I peek up at Jack. Larger than life Jack. He winks at me. "Best. Chocolate. Ever."

Jack holds back on any public displays of affection during dinner, and I'm grateful. This is all still too new and nerve-wracking for me to want to be in everyone's face about it. We enjoy an amazing dinner, pick up a fresh stash of turtles, and head to his truck not having done more than hold hands.

He lets me in on the passenger side and when he shuts the door, something inside me lets out a big breath. My eyes are locked on Jack though. My heart is picking up its pace as I watch that man walk around to the driver's side. Right before he opens the door, I impulsively scoot to the middle.

He gets in and grins at me, looking pleasantly surprised. He puts his arm around me. "Well, hey there, Shorty."

But I don't say anything back. All of a sudden, I'm a girl on a mission. I put my hand on his face and give him an eager kiss.

I need him. I need him right now.

And I kiss him like it. In a matter of seconds, he's kissing me the same way. His other hand comes to my face and his arm pulls me in closer. Our tongues dive in and circle each other, tasting and going deep and needing more and more. Hanging on to him and not breaking our kiss, I come up on my knees and lean over him. Our holds on each other tighten. We come up for air, panting, and he kisses and sucks on my jaw, my neck, my collarbone. I need to wrap my legs around him. I need to feel him coming inside me.

I regret starting this here, in the parking lot, when this is as far as we can go. We pull back slightly, locking eyes. He looks ready to devour me. <u>Not if I devour you first, buddy.</u>

"Let's go to your place," I whisper hotly. It's closer than mine, but also, for some reason I like the idea of being in Jack's bed.

Still giving me that hungry look, he puts the keys in the ignition and starts up the engine. I fall down onto the seat and buckle up, my eyes on him too.

The drive back feels even longer than the drive in, but not for the same reason. I wedge right up next to him, my shoes kicked off and my bare feet tucked up on the seat to my side. My hand is running along his firm chest, his arms, his thighs, his stiff bulge. My chin is resting on his shoulder and I'm looking up at his profile, occasionally kissing his shoulder, neck, cheek, but mostly keeping my eyes on him.

Jack is a wonder to me, and I can't stop taking him in.

He has one hand on the wheel and one arm around me. He's rubbing my back, sides, hips, arms. My skin tingles when he brings his fingertips to the back of my neck and caresses the base of my hair. I tingle even more when he slides his hand under my arm to come around and squeeze my breast. Eventually, he advances down to my ass and is soon reaching from behind so he can stroke my throbbing mound. I can't for the life of me remember why I'm wearing pants instead of a skirt.

Once we're back in town, we get caught at a few red lights. Jack takes those opportunities to remove his hand from the wheel and come at me properly. The only thing keeping me from climbing right into his lap is the damned seatbelt. Each time, it takes someone honking behind us to realize the light's turned green.

When we pull up to his condo, we have our seatbelts undone before the truck even comes to a stop. As he climbs out, he grabs my hand and I grab my shoes. He leads me up the walk barefooted. He's so eager he's half a stride in front of me, but he's got a firm grip on my hand and I'm hustling along too. I'm not going anywhere. He stops to unlock the door and I bump up against him, hanging onto his hand and watching impatiently as he fumbles with the lock.

The door swings open at last and he pulls me inside the darkened room, kicking the door shut and backing me up. I drop my shoes and throw my arms around his neck. He lifts me up, hooks my legs around his waist, and presses me hard against the door. His rock hard bulge hits me right between the legs.

"Yes," I say, clinging to his back. He presses his hard dick against me. Then does it again. I gasp and tilt my head back against the door. Given this opening, he sucks on the tender skin at the base of my neck. I shudder everywhere, letting out a low moan.

"I want you," I say, gasping again as he once more thrusts his cock against me. "Jack, please." Enough fucking around. I need him in me for real.

He pulls back enough to set me on my feet. We take to removing our clothes, but are doing it in between hungry kisses. At last my bra goes flying and my panties are the last item of clothing remaining. Leaving my panties on, Jack turns his attention to my breasts. He squeezes, licks, sucks, and pulls. I'm rubbing my hands down his bare back, angling my hips and legs toward him, asking for more.

Finally, Jack starts to slide off my panties, dropping to one knee. He tosses the panties aside, but stays down and holds me firmly against the door by the hips. I watch him dive into me. He teases my lips open with his tongue. I grab onto his strong forearms for support when he slides over my clit.

I lock my knees to keep from falling and throw my head back. I'm still bowled over by everything Jack, still tumbling downstream, but this time I'm not even trying to find anything to hang onto. I'm gasping and panting and gripping the hair on the back of his head as he eats me into sweet oblivion.

There's no holding back the sounds I want to make this time. He strums my clit hard and I cry out, not able to contain it.

"There she is," Jack says, before swirling the wet flat of his tongue over my clit. A long, high cry escapes me as he sets my entire body on fire. "Mmmmmm," he rumbles, his mouth fully on me and the vibrations from his voice trembling through me.

"Damn, Jack," I gasp. My knees are starting to give way as my body starts that delicious climb to climax. "Oh fuck."

He lifts one leg so my thigh is resting on his shoulder. I let him support my weight and start to curl forward, bracing myself on his arm and shoulder.

He hardens his tongue and starts flicking rapidly over my clit. "Yes," I gasp. "Yes, yes."

Then I'm past talking as I climb high and hard. My other knee starts to give but Jack's giving me enough support. I'm shuddering and gasping, clutching him hard, as the hot pleasure in my core blooms outward. It sweeps over my chest and face, spiking higher and higher in the center where Jack's working me. I cry out over and over as Jack pushes me higher and higher until the pleasure tears through me and I'm gripped in an orgasm so powerful I can only roll my head and pant frantically.

The waves crash over me, causing my body to tremble. Now Jack knows exactly what it sounds like when I'm released and not holding back. Based on the noises he's making, I'm thinking he likes it, which increases my pleasure that much more.

When I start to release and my body weakens, Jack comes up and catches me in his arms. We're on the move now, Jack carrying me with my legs wrapped around him. This again. I love it when he carries me like this. Caressing him, I kiss his shoulder and neck.

He takes me to a room I've rarely been in: his bedroom. I tuck my head around so I can take it all in: the heavy, dark-wood headboard. The thick, black comforter. The satin pillowcases.

It's always been Jack's little man cave, but everything about being here with him feels like coming into a safe shelter.

He lays me on the bed and goes quickly to his nightstand. I watch him watching me as he deftly puts on a condom. Again, I have to resist the urge to tell him not to. I want him raw.

"The things I'm going to do to you," he says in a low, sexy voice I feel all the way to my core.

"Yes, please."

As he climbs onto the bed to join me, Tsunami Jack makes a reappearance. His presence is almost more than I can handle. He rolls me onto my side, bends my legs, and kneels right next to me with his knees spread wide, entering me from behind. He'd lifted my top knee slightly so he could slide into me easier, but now that he's in, he presses my knee back down so my legs are pinned together. The pressure of his massive shaft sliding in and out of me ignites a new fire deep inside me.

Again, I'm moaning helplessly.

"That's my girl," he says thickly, looking at me with blazing eyes, "Let me hear those sexy noises you make."

As if I could stop now.

His cock is lighting up every inch of me as he rocks me rhythmically. His angle puts extra pressure on my side wall, something I love. He's almost found my favorite position already. Then he lifts my top leg to rest it on his nearest shoulder, and holds my thigh against his chest as he straddles my bottom leg. The whole time his thick cock stays inside me, and now he's found my favorite position.

"Ahhhh, yes," I say. "I love that."

Now he's able to pump faster and deeper. He braces himself against the headboard with one hand, biceps flexing, leaning over me more and bringing my top leg with him, spreading me wider. His cock is angling hard against my side wall, causing pleasure to bloom outward from that spot over and over again. I feel a drop of moisture escape me and run down my seam.

"You're so wet," Jack says thickly, looking at me with an astonishing mix of passion and tenderness as he rams me hard. I didn't know it was possible to experience all this at once.

Then our eyes lock in a new way. Every sensation in my body and heart magnifies. I look at him looking at me, his body over me, him inside me, and we're joined body and soul. All of a sudden it's too much, too much, too much but I don't want him to stop, either. His fingers slide down my thigh, heading for my mound. His fingers touch my sensitive bud and the jolt zips through my entire body. All the while, his eyes grip mine and I'm tumbling and helpless and overpowered by love for him.

I can't speak. I can't look away. I can only gasp and pant and whimper as he brings me to another shattering climax. I clutch at his thigh and close my eyes and throw my head back and come undone. His hardness enters me again and again, and his fingers strum me rapidly, and I cry out helplessly.

At last I'm released. When he pulls out of me and lets my body rest heavily on the bed, I'm trembling. He's still kneeling, but now he's rubbing his hands firmly up my thighs, up my stomach, up my chest, then back down. He's grounding me and getting me ready for more. His cock is so hard I can see the strain in it. He's watching me and I'm too captured to do anything but watch him back.

He's hungry for me, but I'm already consumed.

Too much. It's too much, Jack. Have mercy on me.

But when he comes down on top of me, I open my arms and pull him into a willing embrace. He enters me and I am a little boat on a big ocean. I tilt my head back and close my eyes and let Jack take me to a place I've never been. I'm helpless to stop it. His breath is hot on my neck and his arms firm around me. Jack rocks me. He sends my little boat over the waves, higher and higher. Just like this, head back, eyes closed. My body is his to command and I am hot with his wishes. A gentle and powerful swell rises in me. He is everywhere in me and I am everywhere in him. Jack rocks me. Bigger and bigger. More and more.

Have mercy.

This is not an emerging climax of the body, but an emerging climax of the soul. And when it explodes inside me, and I'm trembling with ecstasy, and Jack is releasing and shuddering over me, I am finally, fully acquainted with the great and terrible power of love.

Chapter 20

Jack

I know I've got a skittish little doe on my hands. Don't think I don't.

On our date, I was careful to call her to me gently and not do anything to startle her. Then she startled me when she kissed me in the truck like that. And asked for more. And kept that fire burning all the way home and into my bedroom.

Sam's a force to be reckoned with, for sure.

But it got away from both of us, there at the end, and I can only hope I haven't frightened her back into the woods.

In fact, I'm kind of regretting the timing of the big dinner we have to go to tonight. It's a fancy dinner at The Iron House to celebrate the conclusion of Ashley and Erik's summer tour, and everyone's going to be there. All the girls, and all their guys.

And Sam and I.

I don't know if Sam's ready for this. I'm tempted to text everyone and tell them to behave. I'd keep the whole thing under wraps, if I could, but I sort of blew my chances at that when I kissed Sam the way I did right in front of Ashley.

Not that I regret that.

It was soooo worth it.

When I pull up to Sam's house, she doesn't come out to meet me. I'm not sure if that's progress or not. When I go inside, she's not in the immediate vicinity so I holler out, "Hey Shorty. You ready?"

She emerges from the hallway—wearing one of my favorite dresses of hers, the slim, blue number—pointing to the phone she's holding to her ear and rolling her eyes. "I know, Mom, but there's nothing you can do about that now."

I grin. Ah, her mom. She's a bit of a mess, but she's got a good heart.

"Mom, I—" Sam drops her phone half an inch, rolls her eyes, and sighs. I can see now she's legitimately frustrated about something. But about what? If she's talking to her mom, it could be anything.

I hear her mom's voice, but can't make out of much of what she's saying. She sounds like she might be crying. What's going on?

We sort of drift deeper into the living room and end up sitting on the couch as Sam continues to listen and starts trying to calm her mom down. She looks at me and mouths, "Sorry."

I nod. It's okay.

After about fifteen minutes, I've sent Ashley a text letting her know we'll be a bit late and pieced together what's going on. It sounds like Sam's mom is on her way to getting divorce number four. Great.

Finally her mom's calmed down and Sam's trying to wrap things up. Then her mom says something that rubs Sam wrong, because she straightens and gets a hard look on her face. Her mom is still talking, but Sam stands abruptly, grabs her purse off the table, and gives a quick gesture toward the door that means, <u>Let's just get the fuck out of here.</u>

I follow Sam out, phone still to her ear. "Well, we'll talk more later, Mom, okay?" Her voice is tight and I have a feeling she's about to go nuclear about something. We get to my truck and I open the door for her. I take her nearest hand, as well as her other arm, and give her some support. It wouldn't be the first time I've helped Sam climb into my truck in a nice dress and heels, so we manage it without forethought or comment.

When I get in myself, Sam's saying, "I'm sorry, but I have to go. We have that dinner... No, it's fine. You're fine. We'll talk later... Okay, bye."

She pulls the phone away from her ear, taps disconnect with her thumb, and chucks it onto the seat between us.

"Fucking hell."

"She and Derek are splits, huh?"

Sam's got her arms crossed now. She just grunts.

"Is she okay?"

"Peachy."

I sigh. "What happened?"

"Oh, you know," she tosses her hands up. "Derek is up to his old tricks and mom just can't understand it." Sam says this in her mocking voice, rolling her eyes. "You know, because she loves him so much, or what the fuck ever. Well, this time he's the one ending things, and it's just as well, because otherwise Mom would just hang on in that mess forever before finally getting up the balls to leave him." Sam exhales sharply. "You know what she said to me?"

I don't know if I want to know.

"She says he was such a great guy at first." Sam gives me a withering look. "As if. She couldn't spot a great guy if you knocked her upside the head with one. I called it, didn't I? I knew it clear back when they were dating this was how it was going to end, but she was too fucking in love with that asshole to see it."

Yeah. I'm definitely not saying a word right now. She just needs to blow off some steam and I'm going to sit here and let her.

But Sam surprises me.

Instead of going off on things further, she folds her arms and looks out the passenger window. I wouldn't worry about it if she looked merely pissed. Hell, she could just be taking a breather in between rants. No biggie.

But the look on her face, I admit, it has me worried. She looks thoughtful, and I don't think she's thinking about her mom anymore.

Fuck.

We're practically to The Iron House, and I'm not so sure Sam's in the right frame of mind for a dinner party. "Do you still want to go? I could take you home."

She frowns at me. "I'm not missing this. Why would I do that to Ashley?"

"Okay." I look forward, giving her some space. "Just checking."

Sam takes a deep breath. I glance over and see she's trying to get herself together. I give her a few more minutes, letting her put her phone in her purse in silence. "Sorry," she says tightly.

"For what?" I say lightly, trying to coax her into a better place.

She sighs, and says nothing.

Yeah, okay. It's not a time for jokes.

I pull into the parking lot and find a spot. I kill the engine, but neither one of us moves. "Hey," I say gently. She won't look at me. "Hey," I say again.

This time she looks over. I'm not sure what to think about what I see. I really don't know what she's thinking. "Are you okay?"

She shrugs. "I didn't care about the guy."

"That's not what I meant."

She sighs, folding her arms again and looking out the windshield. "Mom'll be fine eventually," she says dully. "She's been through it before."

"That's not what I meant either."

She doesn't move, but her brows furrow together and her face slowly softens. "I'm okay," she says, softer now. "Let's just... have a good time for Ashley's sake, okay?"

She looks at me then. "Say something funny."

I raise my eyebrows. "No pressure or anything."

"I don't want to carry this shit in there."

I reach over and open the glove box. "Then put your shit in there. If that doesn't work, I'll fuck your brains out right here in this truck until you're screaming in ecstasy."

She gives me a wry look. "Would that be for your benefit, or mine?"

I give her a sly smile and she blushes. God, I love that. She shuts the glove box and sticks her tongue out at me.

I grin. That's my girl.

Thankfully I got to Sam's house early enough that we're only about ten minutes late to the restaurant, but everyone's already here and gathered at a big, round table in one of The Iron House's rear dining rooms. I'm bracing myself for some smart aleck comments about the fact that Sam and I are here together, but no one says a word about it. Not that we're exactly giving them easy ammunition—I'm not holding Sam's hand or pulling out her chair or really doing anything differently at all—but still, I figured we'd get some sort of shit when we got here. All that happens is Ashley gives us an appraising look, and Chloe and Isabella exchange what they think are sneaky grins, and that's it.

I'm pretty proud of them. And grateful. Because Sam could use a breather right now. Honestly, I could too.

We've finished hearing the latest updates from Ashley and Erik about their tour—apparently things went successfully enough that their agent is starting to book them into some pretty serious venues for next summer—when Isabella says the last thing I expected to hear.

"So, Jack, how are things going with Emily?"

We're in the starter course, so I'm conveniently swallowing some French onion soup when Bella asks me that. Now I'm not so conveniently choking on it and coughing and wondering what in the fuck's going on.

Shane's sitting next to me and gives me a couple hearty whacks on the back as I reach for my water. I'm not too distracted to notice Ashley and Sam exchanging uncomfortable glances.

Wait a minute. Ashley hasn't said anything? The other girls don't know? Now that I think about it, I guess they probably would've texted me if they did. But... that means Sam hasn't told them either.

Why not?

I'm looking at her as I'm downing my water, but she's struggling to maintain her composure too.

"You okay?" Isabella asks me.

No.

I nod and clear my throat. "We broke up." And I will never say one more word about that, in case you were wondering.

Isabella and Chloe grin at each other and then look at Sam.

Okay, something's up. Do they know or not? Maybe this is their way of messing with us, but they just don't know enough to leave Emily out of the conversation?

"Um..." Sam pinches her eyes closed and scratches the base of her neck.

'Um' is right. What do I say? Sam and I are hooking up? Sam and I are going out? (Not that we've really discussed things enough to define it, what with her being a skittish doe and all.) Or do I say the truth, which is I'm hopelessly in love with her and going to do everything in my power to marry her and keep her forever. If I can pull it off.

"We're kind of..." Sam weakly gestures between the two of us, "trying things."

Okay, I can live with that for now, and at least she's the one who said it. But there's no containing the reaction around the table, especially from Isabella and Chloe.

"Well, it's about damned time," Isabella says, grinning.

Chloe has her hands clasped to her chest. "Oh my god!"

"Chloe," Sam says lowly, rolling her eyes.

"Oh my god!" Chloe says again.

"Will you please not do that?" Sam's acting like her normal self, but not. I sense the tension underneath.

I'm with you, girl. I'm not comfortable either.

"What's that mean, 'trying things'?" Grayson asks.

I give him a look. Thanks, Grayson. Thanks a <u>lot.</u> He grins at me.

Okay, time to take things in a different direction and get back some control. "You know," I say lightly, "trying things. Missionary. Doggie style. Reverse cowgirl."

Sam gapes at me; everyone else is starting to laugh, though.

"Splitting bamboo," I continue.

"Alright, that's enough," Sam says and everyone laughs. She's grinning a bit, too, and I take a big breath. Okay, one hurdle down. Let's move on to something else, shall we?

I ask Isabella how things are going with her job. After a few good-natured jabs about me trying to change the subject, they finally let it go and we all listen to Isabella getting us caught up on things.

But the situation isn't as under control as I thought. As we move through the evening, no one can seem to resist interrupting the current topic of conversation to take the occasional jab at either Sam or me about this new development in our relationship. It's harmless, really, except that it's not. I know they don't know what they're doing, because Sam is doing a pretty admirable job shrugging it off (I'm doing my best, too), but I can sense the tension in her rising and rising.

Meanwhile, my thoughts keep returning to one potential problem: Sam didn't tell a soul. Why not? Was she keeping a back door open for herself so she could more easily escape?

I admit, the whole thing has me a little on edge.

Grayson asks who wants to join the football pool he's got going with some friends, then Isabella pipes in and says they need a pool to see who can guess how long it'll be before Sam and I tie the knot.

Bloody hell.

I glance sharply at Sam. I don't like the look on her face. Not at all.

"I want in on that action," Chloe says gleefully.

But I'm worn out and I've had enough and I really need them to stop pushing her.

"Knock it off, ladies," I say, in a tone that silences the entire table.

Chapter 21

Sam

Everyone's staring at Jack in stunned silence, but I doubt anyone's more stunned than I am. There was something raw in Jack's voice that got my full attention. I look at him, really look at him for probably the first time this entire evening. Instantly, my heart softens. I think I've been too caught up in my own panic to realize something: Jack's frightened, too.

Of losing me.

"Wow," Grayson says quietly, clearly impressed. "I think Jack just busted out his dad voice."

God, I know. It's totally sexy and a little overwhelming, like fucking everything about Jack is these days. But I spare barely a glance for Grayson and the others. I'm only looking at Jack.

"Just lay off, all right?" he says, easier now, trying to lighten the mood a bit so everyone can move on.

But I can't move on yet, not with Jack looking so alone. He shouldn't feel alone when I'm sitting right next to him. As I think about what I want to do, my heart swoops into my chest, a big ball of nerves. But I take a deep breath, put both hands on Jack's face, pull him down to me, and kiss him right in front of everybody.

I feel the shock in his body. I sense the shock around the table. I'm shocked, too. But I hang on until he's pressing his lips back against mine. I hold him for another couple seconds, then release him.

His eyes are soft and loving and grateful.

I give him a wink, then pick up my glass of wine and sweep my eyes around the table. "So suck it." With trembling hands I drink my wine until there's not a drop left.

By the time we're back in the truck, I'm past exhausted. I end up telling Jack I need him to just drop me off at home. I know full well what will happen if he comes in, and I need space to breathe. I really do. But I hold his hand and try to reassure him that it's nothing he did. He only gives me that easy-going smile of his and tells me he understands and that he'll stalk me with texts tomorrow until I let him come over again.

That boy makes me smile. I almost change my mind and let him come in after that, but we say our goodnights.

I lie in bed thinking for a long time, before finally falling asleep.

The next morning, I text Jack: Carpet's on sale at Lowe's. Wanna come?

Jack: Can we get hot dogs from the hot dog cart?

Me: Only if you're a good boy.

I can just see his evil grin.

Jack: You betcha. *fingers crossed behind back*

Me: You can come over whenever.

Jack: I'll be right there.

In the past, 'whenever' really meant whenever. It might be a couple hours before I'd see him and it wasn't a big deal. This time, I'm glad there won't be a wait, because I need to get this over with. Ever since that morning Ashley caught us, I've been thinking about what she said, and she's right.

Jack and I need to talk.

I meant to do it right away, but then decided the carpet section at Lowe's probably wasn't the place. Still, I ordered new carpet for the living room and Jack got his hot dog, so there was that at least.

Then I meant to do it when we were having Panda Express for lunch (because "hot dog" means "a wee snack" in Jack speak). Instead we ended up joking about pointless fortunes that aren't really fortunes and making water snakes with our straw wrappers.

I really, really meant to do it before Jack and I started in again. But we've been back at my place something like a minute and a half and we're already going at it.

Because I can't help myself.

Because he is hands-down the hottest man I've ever been with, and a force of nature I can't resist, and the only one who's ever cracked my heart wide open like this.

And we really, really need to talk.

Instead, he's got me pinned against the living room wall and I can't get enough of him. He's kissing me eagerly, holding my rear and bringing the front of my shorts hard against his cock. I'm diving deep in his mouth, whimpering in my need for him.

I fumble with his shirt, hurriedly bringing it up. He lifts his arms so I can take it off. At the sight of his bare chest, I want to taste his skin and suck on his nipples. I don't have the chance, because he's lifting my shirt now. I bend my knees, so he's half removing my shirt and I'm half sinking out of it. As soon as my arms are free, I hang onto his sides, his bare skin hot under my hands, and start kissing his chest.

His hands come around me, softly cradling my head and my back. When I move to his firm nipple and take it in my mouth, he groans and holds me firmer. I suck on him slowly, running my tongue around his nipple. My hands are caressing his back and chest, and he's caressing me too, breathing hard. I work my way to the other side, tasting him as I go. I slowly run my hand down his stomach, then lower. When I reach his other nipple and suck on it firmly, I squeeze his hard shaft at the same time, right through his jeans.

He groans and I start working my way down, planting kisses on his stomach as my hands start working his jeans, unfastening everything until he's released and throbbing right in front of me. When I take his cock into my mouth, sucking and working him with my tongue as I slide down, he sucks his breath in through his teeth and leans forward heavily, catching himself against the wall.

"God, Sam."

I take him in deeply, working his shaft with my mouth and one hand as I pull his jeans down with the other. Soon he's in front of me in all his naked glory, and I'm practically making love to his cock. I wrap my arms around his thighs, embracing him, then around his ass, squeezing. He's panting hard now and I'm throbbing. I'm still in my bra and shorts (yet again, why aren't I wearing a skirt?) and naked Jack is panting and groaning above me, holding me firmly by the back of the head and starting to thrust into me.

That's right baby, come at me. I can take it.

His dick is so tight I'm able to lightly use my teeth and he only groans more. I'm so turned on just from sucking him off, it wouldn't take much to send me over. I'm torn between wanting him to come in my mouth and wanting to get this amazing cock between my legs where it belongs.

Jack makes the decision for me.

He pulls me into a stand and plants such a firm kiss on my mouth I'm practically slammed against the wall. Next thing I know,

278

he's yanking my shorts down to my ankles. As he takes care of my panties too, I remove my bra myself. When he comes back up, his hungry look grips me and I know I'm about to be tumbled downstream again.

He saves me, though, when he impatiently turns me so I'm facing the wall, his warm body against mine. His hard cock is right against the fleshiest part of my ass. <u>Oh yeah, baby. This'll do just fine.</u>

"Oh wait," he says tightly, and I instantly know what he's thinking.

He only has time to move half an inch before I stop him with a desperate "No! Forget it." I want him raw.

He doesn't argue. He wraps one arm around my shoulders, bends his knees slightly, and tucks his mouth next to the back of my neck. His other hand has a hold of his cock, the tip of which is against my folds, seeking. I open my legs more and arch my hips back, giving him easier access. When his tip finds my entrance, I exhale in anticipation. "There, baby," I whisper. But he already knows.

He firmly presses against me until the tight ring of my opening gives way and he's sliding in. Deeper and deeper. Raw, and all Jack. Still holding me, he braces his other hand against the wall. Both of us panting, we're still, allowing my body to open, then relax and grip him firmly. Then he begins. Slowly at first. Each ridge of his cock rubs against every ridge in my body.

"Yeeeees," I breathe.

Still slowly pumping me, he grabs one breast and squeezes it firmly, massaging it. "Yes." I turn my head slightly toward him. Jack kisses my cheek once, twice, as he starts to pump me faster. My slick channel is on fire, and my clit is humming, aching for touch. I rest my hand on his as he squeezes my breast. I keep it there as he moves over and squeezes the other one. He's still driving into me, harder and faster. I arch back more to meet him, pinching my eyes closed and letting my mouth gape open.

My hand is still on his as he starts to slide it down my stomach and toward my mound. I push him slightly, eager, and he complies by moving his hand faster. When his fingers slip over my clit, my fingers still on top of his, I arch my head back and cry out and still he's pumping me.

"Yes, Jack, yes. Don't stop." This is exactly what I want.

His arm that was against the wall comes down then and grips my body hard against his as he increases his rhythm, faster and faster. I bring my arms in front of me, bent in front of my chest, and use them to brace against the wall as he leans harder into me.

"Ohmigod."

"Damn, you feel good," he says tightly, his hot breath in my ear. "Oh, Sam."

He's thrusting hard into me, his tongue teasing my earlobe, his finger rubbing my clit in short, rapid motions. I'm arching back against him, my face and chest hot and flushed. I'm past words, and letting out my low sex cries over and over. I'm so overwhelmed with pleasure, my mind feels tipped to the edge of insanity.

I can't even breathe as I feel myself climbing. The heat in my body peaks, the pleasure ballooning within me peaks, the tsunami of ecstasy peaks and I am trembling and crying out as my orgasm tears through me. Jack moans loudly in my ear as he comes too.

I gasp and cry out over and over, panting hard and shuddering as he climaxes against me. He's crushing my breast as he holds me tight, moaning in my ear, and my orgasm eats me alive. <u>God, yeeeeeees.</u>

At last, my body is released from the mind-numbing high and I gasp for breath, leaning harder against the wall, losing the ability to support myself. After he slows and comes out, he leans gently against me, cradling me. We're both panting hard, slowly stilling. My body is still humming.

He eases off me just enough to turn me to face him. I keep my eyes closed and tuck my face into his chest, trying to catch my breath. <u>I love you, I love you, I love you.</u>

Which reminds me. We really do need to talk.

After locking the front door to prevent unexpected interruptions, and noting that we should probably make a habit of that from now on, we move to the bedroom and rest under the covers.

The moment is now. I know it is. We're on our sides, facing one another, limbs entangled and hands lightly caressing faces, shoulders, arms. My heart is pounding out of my chest, and not from anything physical we're doing. It's from the knowledge that if I want to not fuck this up, I have to be willing to do it right. I have to be willing to talk to him.

That knowledge is doing nothing to keep me from feeling terrified.

I spit it out before I can stop myself. "What are we doing, Jack?"

He waggles his eyebrows at me.

Geez, he's such a dork. "I mean, I know what we're <u>doing</u>." He grins, but I'm serious. "But what are we doing? What is this?"

Jack's eyes soften and he grows serious, too. He comes up on his elbow, looking down at me, making my heart all fluttery. He's considering me. Part of me thinks he might not want to say what this is. What if it's so much more for me than it is for him? I mean, I know enough to know this isn't a casual fling. I get it. But I also know us humans of the female persuasion tend to fall for guys long before they fall for us. Maybe it's the way we're wired, I don't know, but I've seen it happen over and over again. So, yeah, the thought that I'm the only one losing control here makes me more than a little nervous.

But... that's not why I've been avoiding this conversation. Not at all. There's something far more terrifying Jack could say.

"I'll answer that question for you if you'll answer one for me."

"Okay." I'm trying to be grown up about this and not sound as scared as I feel.

"Is it a deal?"

I nod.

"Okay." He takes a deep breath. "You want to know exactly how I feel about you, is that it?"

I nod again, even more nervous now. Here we go.

"That's fair enough. But... I don't want to freak you out. All right?"

Too late for that, dude. I nod, barely.

He looks at me, his eyes softening. I fall into them. Just like that, I'm surrounded by Jack. How is he doing this to me?

He takes another breath, then says softly, "I'm in love with you, Sam."

My breath hitches in my chest and my eyes widen. My heart's beating soundly. Here it is. Another line we can't ever uncross and Jack just went galloping right over it. Why did I make him do that?

I know I should say something. I should. I should tell him I love him, too. I should. But I'm freaking the hell out, just like he knew I would.

What in the hell is wrong with me?

Still holding me with those soft eyes, he caresses my cheek and says, "I'm so crazy, hopelessly in love with you."

God, he said it again. How can he just come out and say it like that?

"So," he says, holding my eye. "Time for you to answer my question."

I can only blink at him. Uh-oh.

"Why did you say you were sorry?" he asks.

Huh?

That's not the question I was expecting. Sorry about what? What's he talking about?

I relax for a second, thinking he gave me a safe, easy question. Then suddenly, I know what he's talking about. I know <u>exactly</u> what he's talking about.

It was that night, when he found me crying on the coffee table. It all started because he said if he didn't know better he'd think I was crying over a boy, and my reaction made it so obvious that I was.

I remember the moment he's asking about so clearly: me on the coffee table, Jack lying on the floor under me, me looking at him and realizing I couldn't hide the fact that I was one more girl he made fall in love with him.

Fall in love with him.

That's when I said, "Sorry." I said it because I was sorry I fell in love with him.

Dammit, he knows it too.

"No lying," he says softly, because of course my realization about the sneaky-ass question he just asked is all over my face.

I scowl at him and he starts to grin.

Oh, hell.

"Because..." I start.

His grin gets slowly wider. "Yes?"

Oh, hell, hell, hell.

I take a deep breath. "Because I kind of, you know..." I purse my lips and pinch my eyes shut, "love you, too."

I peek one eye at him. He's wearing the biggest Jack grin I've ever seen. "Ah, Sammy," he says in his teasing voice, pulling me in, "That's so sweet. So tender."

"Shut up."

He kisses me then. And kisses me. And I'm kissing him back because I am officially hopeless. In a matter of seconds, I'm sinking into the mattress and he's washing me away. That's when it hits me what he said. He loves me. My heart swells so high and so fast it feels like it's going to burst. He loves me. Thank God, thank God.

He pulls away, still smiling. I'm just trying to breathe. Man alive. Being in love is so fucking <u>intense.</u> I give him a smile too, though. I'm starting to see why people risk everything for this.

"I love making you melt."

"I did not melt," I protest, but I'm smiling because I've never seen that boy look so happy. Did I do that?

"Making you melt is almost better than making you come," he says, still grinning.

"Well, that's debatable."

"I said almost." He draws me in closer and hitches my leg over his hip, his eyes getting that heated look that lights me up all over. "But we could try it again if you're not sure."

Chapter 22

Sam

Then this happens.

It's a Saturday afternoon, a week later, and I'm enjoying a perfectly lazy day, watching <u>French Kiss,</u> and waiting for Jack to get out of the local one-day conference he's attending. I'm getting a little more comfortable with the idea that love is wild and slightly out of control, but also incredible and fucking worth it and maybe, just maybe, something I can handle.

Perhaps those are the thoughts that are distracting me as I get up to answer the hard knock at the door. I don't even peek through the window to see who it is.

When I open the door to see my dad standing there, my blood drops clear to the floor.

I suddenly remember that text mom sent me almost three months ago, clear at the beginning of summer when Jack and I were at the beach. That was the first and last I heard and I eventually forgot all about it. I let my guard down. I swear, he knows. I swear to God, it's like he does it on purpose, just to fuck with me and pretend he's not.

He almost looks the same as the last time I saw him. Same hard gray blue eyes, same thick arms knotted with muscle, same half-moon scar over his left eyebrow that he got in the accident all those years ago. But he looks more rough and hollowed out—most likely the result of four more years of hard drinking since I saw him last—and his two-day stubble is flecked with more gray.

How did you find me?

"Ah, there's my Samantha," he says in that harsh jovial tone I think he thinks is supposed to be fatherly. My parents are the only ones who call me Samantha and my dad is the reason I hate it.

"Dad," I manage to spit out. He steps across the threshold. My skin is crawling with dread as he throws a hard arm around my neck and gives me a gruff, half hug. He reeks of body odor and whiskey. I wonder if he's homeless again. I wonder how much he's had to drink already today.

He lets himself in the rest of the way and I see a motorcycle parked by the curb. I hadn't even heard him coming. I never, ever see this guy coming.

I think about bolting and running barefoot down the sidewalk and down the street and just going and going. Instead, I slowly close the door.

He's walking right into the kitchen. I follow him in silence, feeling a strange mixture of pulsing fear and numbness. Maybe he'll just talk to me for a while and then leave. I just need to not do anything to upset him so he'll go.

He's heading for the refrigerator, but instead of opening it, he cranes his neck to see what's on top.

There's nothing there, but I instinctively know what he's looking for.

"Got anything for your old dad to drink?" he asks. "I'm parched."

"There's juice in the fridge."

He grunts and gives me one of his looks. On the outside, he tries to make it look like he's joking, but on the inside he's saying, <u>Don't fuck with me, girl.</u> "I'm thinking something a little stronger."

I don't want to tell him, but he'll only find it anyway, and then be mad at me for hiding it. "The cupboard next to the stove," I say, pointing.

"Ah." He sidles on over. As my dad opens that cupboard and appraises my stock—half a bottle of whiskey, rum for daiquiris, and the makings for margaritas—I feel dirty for even having it. "That's more like it. I guess you are related to me." He laughs harshly, always so amused at himself.

A sick, crawling sensation slips down my legs.

Okay, I can't. I can't. I can't do this. Why is he here? I can't do this.

I sidestep behind the island, so he can't see me pull out my phone. With fumbling fingers, I send Jack a text: <u>My dad is here.</u>

"Hey!" my dad barks, and I jolt my gaze up to see him watching me. Even though I know he doesn't know what I'm doing and is just irritated I'm not paying full attention to him, I hit the button on the side of my phone to blacken the screen so he can't see what's on it.

"You got a glass?" He holds up the bottle of whiskey he's pulled down as if to say, 'Why do I even have to ask, dumb ass?'

I quickly tuck my phone into my back pocket and get a glass from the cupboard. "You kids these days are always on your fucking phones," he mutters. I don't reply to this. I don't say a word as I watch him fill the glass half full of whiskey. He doesn't look at me as he pours. He never looks at anyone when he pours. He takes a swig then heads into the living room, starting to really look around for the first time. "So you own this place, huh?"

Again, I'm wondering how he knows that and how he found me. Did he call mom when she was having a weak moment and make her break down and tell him? I'd love to be able to say she'd never do that, but he still has power over her too, and her weak moments are plentiful when she's in the middle of a divorce.

"Yeah," I say, as he sinks down onto my couch.

He looks around with a dismissive expression. "It's not much to look at, is it? But it's more than I've ever been able to do." He says that as if it's my fault. "There's no catching a break with luck like mine."

He takes another swig of the stuff that's created the shitty ass "luck" he's got. Meanwhile, I perch on the other end of the couch and look at my house with fresh eyes. I see all the things I've grown used to. The dated lighting fixtures. The old blinds I've yet to replace. The little cracks in the wood at the base of the door. I've even grown used to the pink shag carpet, because this isn't just a little house I bought. It's home and a place I've felt safe and comfortable. But now I see it all through his eyes and it feels dirty and dark.

Like I do.

I wish I were wearing something different. I'm in shorts and a tank, and suddenly feel way too exposed. I hope he doesn't comment on it. I hope he doesn't say that word I hate.

My heart rate suddenly increases because I've just realized Jack can't come because he's at a conference and probably has his phone off anyway. My dad starts telling me about the bike out front—I've no idea why. I take his self-absorption as an opportunity to covertly pull out my phone. I'm trying to think quick—if I contact one of the girls I don't want anyone to come alone—but before I can start a message my dad looks at me and says, "Girl, put that fucking phone away."

I freeze, assessing the look on his face, hunting for the slightest sign of danger. I'm instantly regretting that I've put him between me and the door.

My flashbacks are so vivid, they're squeezing the breath out of my lungs...

...my mother on the floor, in her black shirt with the gold dots, curling away from him and making that high-pitched scream no human should ever have to make

...him straddling her body and punching her so hard in the side the sound of it reverberates through the house

...me huddling on the cold tile floor, under the kitchen table, hands pressing so hard over my ears and still hearing it all anyway

...the ceramic shards of the plate on the floor next to me, smears of spaghetti sauce on the white and blue ceramic pieces

It had all happened so fast, too. Five minutes earlier, you never would've guessed.

"I didn't raise you to be so fucking rude," he says now.

"Sorry." I slide my phone back into my pocket.

He eyes me hard, as if trying to decide if I'm sorry enough. I don't move a muscle. He snorts and drinks down the rest of his whiskey in one shot. "Here." He shoves the glass in my direction. "Get me a refill."

I take it and go into the kitchen for more, obedient daughter that I am.

Throughout my life, I've sort of against my will ended up in conversations with

people who, for some reason I can't comprehend, start telling me about an alcoholic parent they have. I'm always kind of stunned by what they tell me. One girl's father never beat anybody or had rages or got pulled over for drunk driving or passed out in the hallway or anything. He was what she called a "functioning alcoholic," but apparently it was still enough to fuck her up, because her boyfriends were all emotionally-distant addicts of one variety or another anyway.

Another guy said his dad would get fun and loopy when he drank, but couldn't hold down a job, and of course wouldn't stop drinking, and so that's why his mother divorced him. He said he had a "decent" relationship with his dad. They even do holidays and get-togethers.

Fucking Christmas.

I never say what my dad's like. That's locked up tight.

Because apparently even in the world of alcoholic parents, I got the kind that makes people look at you with shock and horror and pity. There's a very short list of people in my life I trust enough to know the truth without looking at me like that.

And right now one of them, thank God, is walking through my front door.

Chapter 23

Jack

When I open the door to Sam's house, the scene almost looks normal at first. She's sitting on one end of the couch, and he's on the other. It could be any cozy family get-together, anywhere in the world. But she's unnaturally still and slightly wide-eyed and he is a dark presence seeping through the entire room.

She gives me a look of shock and relief, but it washes over her in the space of a heartbeat, then is gone. I've seen her plenty freaked out over the past few weeks, but this is fear of a different flavor. My adrenaline's been racing since I got her text, but just the sight of her triggers that primitive thing that dwells deep inside of all decent men.

I make my decision in an instant.

"Get your purse, Sam," I say. Head down, she hops up. Arms tight by her side, she hurries past me and down the hallway toward her bedroom. I set my eyes on the man on her couch.

So this is Sam's dad.

Here's what I know about this guy. When he was still married to Sam's poor mom, he got busted for his first DUI and spent a few months in the county jail. Sam was only seven. When she was ten, he got into the kind of one-car accident only drunks are capable of, securing himself his second offense. Except this time, Sam was in the car with him. She has a scar on the backside of her left arm from getting gashed by the window that busted out during the crash. She was lucky to walk away with no more than that cut and a handful of bruises. Having his ten-year-old daughter in the car while driving drunk bumped up the charges from a misdemeanor, second-offense DUI to a felony with child endangerment. Instead of the county jail, he went to prison for six years. It isn't half of what he deserved.

Sam hasn't seen hide nor hair of him for most of her adult life, and damn near half of her childhood, too. But every time he shows up, it's some sort of shit storm. There was an incident her senior year of high school, a few months after he got out of prison, that I'm not too clear on. He got into an altercation with Sam's mom, apparently, and Sam was there to witness the whole thing. Thank God her grandmother came home. Sam's take-no-shit-from-nobody grandmother called the police, but it sounds like she kicked his sorry ass out herself so the police didn't have much to do once they got there. I have no idea how she did it. Sam's mother apparently could've, and should've, pressed charges, but refused. Sam won't talk much about that day—one of the few things she doesn't discuss with me—so I can only imagine what the fuck really went down.

Then there was the time he showed up when we were all still in college. I wasn't there for it, but the girls saw. Isabella ended up escorting Sam to class with her asshole father following along, acting like he thought he had a right to be there. Then he disappeared like he does and that's been that. Isabella told me how Sam had reacted to the whole thing, but I couldn't for the life of me picture the frightened, intimidated Sam that Isabella had described.

As far as I'm concerned, the only thing this sorry excuse for a man did right was this: he brought Sam into the world.

Under normal circumstances, that'd be enough to deserve my respect. I'll make an exception in this case.

"Who are you?" he asks, scrunching his face into a look of detached derision. He strikes me as one of those guys whose default facial expression is to look at you like you're an idiot.

"I'm here to pick Sam up," I say calmly. So get the fuck out.

He gives a harsh bark of a laugh. "Yeah? Where you kids think you're going?" He's slurring his words just slightly. He's taking in my clothes. I'm in slacks, a button-down shirt, and a tie. I left the conference right in the middle of a session about hackers and firewalls.

"We're going to dinner."

"Doesn't that sound nice." The glass in his hand is half full of what looks like whiskey, but he throws it back and it's gone in two seconds flat. Then he looks at me levelly. "I'm hungry. I could eat."

But he doesn't move and I don't think he really wants to come. Based on his hit and run actions of the past, I think all I need to do is get Sam away from him and he'll slink back into whatever slime hole he calls home and she won't see him again for a while. No, I think he's just trying to measure me up.

I debate whether it'd be better to try to get him to leave, or just get Sam out of here and be done with it. I don't know if he'd get into anything with me—weak men who abuse women and children don't always have the balls to stand up to anyone else—but he looks like he might.

He's a short guy, maybe five foot six. I can see where Sam got her height, or lack of it. But he's one of those little guys who try to make up for it in muscle. He's scrappy and tough-looking. He probably knows some good holds, and I imagine he had plenty of opportunity to polish up his fighting skills in prison.

But I doubt he's half as pissed as I am, so I still think I could take him.

The bigger issue is what that would do to Sam. She doesn't need another high-octane experience with this guy. As she hurries back down the hallway, looking for all the world like a terrified little girl, I realize I just need to remove her from the situation as quickly as I can.

The best response to this guy's needling is no response. I maintain eye contact and hold my ground. "Sam, come on." I hold out my arm and gesture with my hand. She hurries to my side. I put my arm protectively around her, but my eyes are on her dad, who's giving me a hard look now.

Yeah, he's definitely not a guy who's afraid to get physical.

"Hey," he says, gruffly, apparently realizing I'm taking Sam whether he approves or not. "I came here to see my daughter."

Too fucking bad. "We're meeting some people." I open the front door and hustle her out in front of me.

"She ain't dressed for it," he says snidely, but I don't respond.

I don't say, 'It was nice to meet you.'

I don't say, 'You can talk to her later.'

I don't bother trying to mask the situation with any bullshit pleasantries because I realize it's pretty obvious I'm escorting her away from him. I can't stomach even pretending it was nice to meet him or that it's okay for him to contact her later. It's not. He needs to be out of her life forever, as far as I'm concerned.

He's starting to get off the couch, and I'd fucking love to have a go at him, but my priority is Sam. I shut the door hard and follow her, catching up with long, smooth strides.

She's hurrying down the sidewalk, shoulders hunched. I put my hand on her lower back. We're almost to the truck when the front door opens behind us.

"Jack—" she says, and my heart breaks at the terror in her voice.

"It's okay."

"Hey!" her dad hollers. I open the passenger door for Sam while giving a quick glance over my shoulder. He's hovering in the open door, scowling but not coming after us. That's a good sign, but I keep my eyes hard on him anyway as she scrambles in and I shut the door.

I go around to the driver's side, and before I get in I hear his parting words: "Fuck you, hot shot!"

Nice.

Clenching my jaw, I start the truck and peel away. Now that we're out of the worst of it, my heart's banging so hard against my ribs it's painful. I'm gripping the steering wheel and wishing I had something to pound. Fucking asshole.

I glance over at Sam. One look at her, and I start to soften, my anger slipping away in hot rivulets as concern for her takes over. "Hey." She's clutching her arms in front of her chest and staring out the windshield with a far-away, frightened look.

"God, you're shaking."

She doesn't respond at all. I examine my rearview mirror to make sure Sam's dad isn't following us, then turn onto a side street and pull over. "Come here, honey," I say, sliding over. She instantly comes to me, crawling right onto my lap and clinging to me.

In the next instant she's sobbing, tearing my heart right out of my chest. She clings to me like she's drowning. Panicked cries shudder through her body.

"You're safe, honey," I say, cradling her. "He's gone. You're safe. It's okay."

But nothing seems to soothe her. Cars rush by, shaking the truck as we're momentarily caught in their airstreams, and Sam just keeps crying. All I can do is hold her. There's nothing I can do to make her pain go away. It's the most helpless feeling I've ever experienced.

After what seems like forever, she starts to settle. Her muscles aren't clenched as tight, but her arms are still hard around me and her head is tucked firmly against my chest. Her crying has settled into sniffling and the occasional, shuddering breath.

Suddenly she lifts her head. "What if he's still in my house?" She's breathing hard, starting to panic again.

"Shh, shh. Let's have someone go by and see."

"Not the girls," she says quickly, as if she's terrified he'd do something to them.

"I'll send Shane, okay? All he has to do is drive by."

She doesn't agree, but she doesn't protest either, huddling back against my chest. Keeping one arm around her, I make a quick phone call to Isabella, but I ask to talk to Shane. Once he's on the phone, I divulge as little as I can while still explaining the situation.

"Tell him not to take Bella," Sam says urgently.

"Sam would rather Isabella not go over there."

"Is he dangerous?" Shane asks, surprised.

I glance at Sam, watching me. "I'd steer clear of him to be safe. Just let us know if he's left or not."

We sit there in silence, waiting, cars still whizzing by. Part of me thinks we need to get back on the road, but the rest of me knows I need to wait. Sam's still clinging to me. She's not going to even begin to unclench until she knows that asshole is out of her house.

And if he's not? I start running through the options. I'm pretty sure he'll leave, but if he's decided to wait around, we may have to take other steps. I think about what that additional drama would do to Sam, and pray he cut and run like he usually does.

At one point she says, "I'm scared to go home."

"You can come home with me, honey." Obviously.

It feels like forever before Shane calls back. "He's gone. His bike wasn't out front, but I checked the house to make sure he wasn't in there. Everything looks in order. We locked it up." I hope Sam didn't hear the 'we' part, because she'll figure out Isabella went anyway, like I knew she would. Thankfully Bella has a key so they could lock the bolt. Not that I think it's likely he'll come back. Chances are, Sam won't see her father again for years.

But that's not really my biggest concern.

My biggest concern is what she does with herself in the meantime. Because I had no idea she had a wound that ran this deep.

By the time we get to my house, she's settled into a grim sort of silence. I get her to eat a little bit, but she won't talk. She just crawls up next to me on the couch and stares into space as I hold her.

It's a little frightening.

Eventually we get ready for bed, but it we're just going through the motions. She doesn't look like she can sleep. Neither could I. It's only when the lights are out, and we're under the covers, and she's huddled against my chest, that she starts to talk low and quiet.

"When I was little," she says, "he had this cigar box on his nightstand."

Then she stops. For a moment, the silence we've felt all evening falls against us again, draping over our skin.

When she goes on, her voice is so soft I have to strain to hear her.

"I liked to look inside it even though I knew I wasn't supposed to. I don't know why. There wasn't anything in it but pennies and his silver lighter and some old receipts."

She pauses again. I'm still, waiting for her.

"One day he caught me looking at it. I think I was... I don't know... five maybe. I remember him storming up to me... So big. I was terrified. I've always wondered what happened after that. I don't remember."

I pull my arms around her tighter. She takes a deep breath and goes on.

"Do you know what I hate most about that night my senior year? After he got out of prison?"

"What?" I ask softly.

"It should be that he was beating the shit out of my mother. I think that time he was trying to kill her. But as horrible as that was, that's not the worst part."

She stops. She stops for so long I don't think she's going to tell me. I squeeze her tighter and rub her arm.

"It was that I didn't do anything to stop it," she says, her voice breaking.

"Ah, Sammy."

"I just sat there," she says, crying again now, "watching him do that to her."

"You were just a kid."

"I was seventeen."

"Like I said."

She shakes her head against my chest, still crying.

"You were a kid," I say firmly, "and even if you weren't the fault lies with him, not you."

"But I think..."

She stops again, unable to say whatever it is she thinks.

"What, sweetheart?"

"I wouldn't stand up to him now either, and I'm not a kid anymore. But—" she chokes down a sob "—I feel like that little girl I used to be every time I'm around him. I... I can't ever seem to stand up to him. I'm just like my mother..."

"You're not."

"I hate how I am around him. I'm so weak. And he makes me feel so... dirty and horrible and worthless."

That bastard.

"And I'm so scared of him. I never know what he's going to do. I'm scared to say anything to make him mad because I don't know what he'll do to me. And I—"

She chokes out a sob again, then says with more venom than I've ever heard in her voice, "I <u>hate</u> him. I fucking hate him."

Then her whole body sort of collapses against me like it's the last thing she has to say and she cries quietly against me. I take a deep breath. "Well," I say gently, "I'm not such a fan myself."

After a while, she starts to settle down and takes a deep breath. "Ugh..." She puts her hand to her forehead and slightly rolls onto her back. "I'm so sick of being blindsided by him. I never know when the fuck he's going to show up."

We lay there quietly for a while, then I say, "Have you thought about getting a restraining order?" Maybe some counseling, too, but now's probably not the time to suggest it.

She sighs. "Yeah, I've thought about it before, but what the fuck is that really going to do? You know how useless those things are? Besides, I'm afraid all that will do is piss him off more and then what will he do?"

"But..." I sigh. "Maybe that's exactly why you need to do it."

She looks at me, bringing her brows together. "What?"

"Well…" I think about how I want to say this. "Honey," I say gently, "you've had a hard time drawing your boundaries around this guy. I think that's the thing that's bothering you the most. I mean, I get that he's an asshole and he's scary. And I'm sorry about that. I really am. You deserve so much better than that. But I think the thing you need to do is discover that you're not as helpless against him as you think you are."

She's looking at me wide-eyed. I rub my hand softly on her shoulder.

"Your dad's always going to be who he is," I say gently. "That's not going to change. But I think you can change how you're coping with it. You can find ways to stand up to him."

"I don't know, Jack. I don't know if I can."

"You can," I say. "Of course, you can."

She sighs and looks up at the ceiling. "So..." she says slowly. "If I file a restraining order and he still shows up, what do I do then?"

She's considering things, and I'm glad for that. I think she needs to come up with this answer on her own though.

"Okay. You've filed an order and he shows up at your house. What would you do?"

She's quiet for a moment, her eyes distant. "I wouldn't have to let him in," she says quietly, "because he already knows I don't want to see him. I don't want him there."

I nod.

"So... I could..." She takes a shaky breath. "I guess I could just close the door or not open it and call the police and let them deal with it."

I nod again, but she's starting to get that frightened look again, and tears are pooling in her eyes. "But what if that's not what he does? What if he sees I got a restraining order and breaks into my house in the middle of the night or something? What if he finds me at work and does something there? What if he gets a gun and goes all postal and we're like those headlines, 'Man kills family, then shoots himself.'?"

"Sam, honey, stop," I say firmly. She lets me pull her in against my chest. "You're going to drive yourself crazy with what ifs like that." It's amazing, how out-of-control our fears can sometimes get. She lets out a shaky breath. "Come on, honey." I squeeze her tighter. "Deep breaths."

She takes a few and eventually settles down again.

After a while I think she's fallen asleep, she's so still and her breathing's so quiet, but then she says softly, "Thank you for being here for me."

"Of course."

"I'm sorry, Jack."

"Sorry for what, honey?"

316

She's quiet. I pull her gently away so I can look at her face. I'm shocked by the pain I see there. "You don't have anything to be sorry about. Geez, Sam."

"But..." she says.

I think she wants to look away, I sense it more than I see it, but I'm holding her eyes. "But what?"

But she stubbornly closes her eyes and tucks back into my chest, and doesn't say any more.

Chapter 24

Sam

I've made Jack a promise.

I told him I would think seriously about getting a restraining order, and that I would definitely get some counseling. I don't really want to talk to a counselor, I'd rather just talk to Jack. I've told him more in the last twenty-four hours than I've ever told anyone, and it helps. But he wants to make sure I don't lock this stuff away again, and I guess he might be right.

Today, he's come home with me. I still haven't decided if I'm sleeping here tonight, or grabbing some clothes and sleeping at Jack's again. He's made it clear I'm always welcome, but he's worried my reasons for staying over there are the wrong ones. He doesn't want me to be afraid of my own house.

It looks strange to me now too, as we come through the front door and into the living room. The place seems changed.

Or maybe it's me who feels that way.

Jack's arm is around me, but in his other hand is a bag of groceries. Our plan is to have dinner and watch a movie. Easy, right? So he says. "Time to claim your house back."

But as I follow him into the kitchen, everything still feels dark and eerie and I wonder if my dad has forever ruined even more parts of me. Not just this house, either. Jack, too.

I watch him pulling out the groceries and I can't help but feel this is more trouble than he should have to go through for me. Why would he want to date a girl who's a pain in the ass, has to file a restraining order against her own father, and needs to promise her boyfriend she'll go to counseling?

Then I see the glass. Someone's put the whiskey bottle away, Shane probably, but the empty glass is next to the sink.

I look at it, and feel a jolt of fear, and instantly I'm pissed by that jolt of fear, and my vision blurs.

"Hey," Jack says gently, seeing me crying once again. And once again, he has to stop his entire world to come over here and comfort me. When he puts his arms up to hold me, I step back.

"No," I say.

He drops his arms and looks at me.

"No," I say again. "It's not fair to you."

"What's not fair to me?"

I exhale sharply, furiously wiping my tears away. "Oh, come on," I say. "I'm fucked up, Jack. I can't do this. You don't want this."

"Hey," he says, firmly. "Don't tell me what I want."

I blink at him, taken back by his tone.

"There's only one thing in the world I want, Sam, and that's you."

"But..." I say, softening but throwing my hands up in exasperation. "Why? Why do you want me? I'm a messed up pain in the ass."

"No, you're not."

"I need fucking <u>therapy</u>."

He laughs.

"Why are you laughing? It's not funny."

"Isn't it?"

I cross my arms. "No."

He's grinning again.

"For God's sake, what?"

"I'll tell you what," he says, a fire in his eye. "I see that little spark coming out in you, and I'm <u>glad</u> because that spark is what you've needed. You think you're weak, Sam, but you're not. You're one of the strongest people I know. Yeah, you've got a wound you need to close, but if you want to know the truth, I think it's pretty fucking amazing you don't have a hell of a lot more."

Something in me softens. Something in me is suddenly desperate to believe what he's saying. Maybe he knows this, because he comes to me and puts his hands on my face. All I can do is put my hands to his sides and hang on.

"Somehow you managed to come out of all that with the most amazing heart and the kind of genuine confidence most people would kill for. You've been living life on your own terms, and look at the life you've built for yourself. You have a great job, your own home, wonderful friends who love you. You. Are not. Your father."

Tears spring to my eyes again.

"And you're not your mother, either. You're <u>you</u>. And you're an amazing person. And I love you more than I knew it was possible to love anybody. And let me tell you something else, Samantha Lawson..."

This stuns me more than anything. He said my name so soft, so gentle, in a way that communicated not just his love for me but his understanding, and his pure acceptance of who I really am. It's the first time in my memory someone has called me by my full name without something inside me cringing. I even... want to hear him say it again. Exactly the way he just said it.

"I am going to love you for the rest of my life," he says, "and there's not one thing you can do about it."

With tears still in my eyes, I go up on tiptoe to kiss him. Then kiss him again. I throw my arms around his neck and hug him and sink into the sensation of him hugging me back. "I love you."

He pulls back and looks at me, smiling.

"I love you," I say again. Then I hold his face and kiss him and say it again. "I love you, Jack Thomas Anderson. I love you so much."

That's the exact moment I start drawing boundaries. I draw a boundary right around Jack and I, and decide I won't let my father touch us. I'm not going to worry about my mother with her string of divorces. I don't care about their mistakes any more. Their mistakes aren't mine, and while Jack might think it's amazing I don't have more wounds, I am only amazed by one thing.

That a girl like me found an incredibly good guy like him.

And I am not letting go.

Chapter 25

Sam

I claim my house back by finally ripping out the old carpet and putting in the new. Then I have all my friends over and we drink and laugh and eat way too much food. Then Jack and I have sex on the new carpet and make love in my own bed with my awesome fucking pillows and I fall asleep tucked into his arms.

With the front door bolted and the new window locks Jack installed for me, but you can understand that, right?

I do my best to clean out and close that big ol' wound from my dad. After a few initial counseling sessions that feel absolutely pointless, I finally start to connect with my therapist and we begin to make progress. First, she gives me permission to grieve the fact that I got stuck with the dad I did and will never have the kind of relationship with him I see my friends having with their amazing dads. That's the first thing. Then I learn to recognize my relationship with him isn't ever going to be something I feel great about, and it may sting and throw me off balance sometimes as I go through life, but he doesn't have to control me so much anymore either. She walks me through mental exercises about how I'll act the next time he resurfaces, which get less and less scary every time I do them. Then she helps me see that there's something hard-wired in us humans to need love and acceptance from our parents, no matter who they are, and she helps me not hurt so much over the fact that I'll never have that from him.

I find a new level of peace inside myself. It's one more scar I'll always carry around, but it's not oozing blood and puss anymore, sorry to be gross about it.

And I just summed up three months of counseling for you. You're welcome.

I did file a restraining order against my dad, and spent about a day feeling a little nervous about it, but mostly I felt empowered. I still do.

And then there's Jack.

Today, I come home from work and walk into my kitchen to find something on the island that stops me in my tracks.

It's a beautiful dragonfly figurine maybe six inches across, with great wings of cut glass and a body of polished silver. I slowly go over and pick it up with both hands, running my thumbs over the smooth wings. Then I notice the little piece of paper it was sitting on. It's a hand-written note that reads: "Be the dragonfly, yo." There's a little arrow indicating I should flip the note over. The back says: "P.S. That cake was delicious."

I look to where the raspberry layer cake used to be and see he's eaten the last piece.

I smile.

In fact, as I look back to the dragonfly, I'm more than smiling. My heart is lifting me right off the ground. Something in me clicks. I feel it. I damn near hear it.

Then I hear the door of Jack's truck close out front.

I set the note and dragonfly on the counter, then hurry through the door to greet the man who understands me better than anyone. There he is, coming up the walk. Tsunami Jack. He still sweeps me away, but I don't fight it any more.

I run and jump into his arms. He laughs and holds me as I wrap my arms and legs around him. He tries to put me down but I hang on. He chuckles and squeezes me hard. "Hey, you. I take it you liked the dragonfly."

I let him put me down, but I stay close, my arms still around his waist, and look up at him. I can't stop smiling, and the way he smiles back at me only makes my heart swell.

I let myself say the words I've felt in my heart for a while now. "Marry me, Jack."

He blinks in shock, but all I can do is look at him earnestly.

"Please," I say. "Make me your wife."

He's still recovering from his shock, but he's starting to grin and getting that light in his eyes I've learned is reserved only for me. "Uh, we're doing this kind of backwards." He holds my face in both his hands.

He's glowing. My Jack is glowing. But I need to hear him say it.

"Propose to me later then. Just say yes first."

He grins and says "Hell, yes" and kisses me before I can even respond. Then kisses me again and again, then we're hugging so tight and he's lifting me up again.

When he sets me down, he says, "Go get your purse," like he has a mission to fill.

I don't argue or ask why. I dash in, grab my purse, and we hustle into his truck.

"Where are we going?" I ask as we're pulling away, me tucked right in next to him.

"My place."

"Uh... my bed's way closer."

He grins at me and I grin back.

"I'm just saying. It's not too late to turn around."

"It's not for that," he says. "Well, not yet."

When we get to his condo, he has me stand in the middle of the living room and points a finger at me, grinning. "Don't move."

I only grin back. Because I'm going to marry that sexy man right there.

He disappears down the hall toward his office. I wait with so much exhilaration, it's flowing off my body and humming in the air.

For the record, I was wrong. Love is amazing.

When Jack comes back, he's wearing an expression of love and excitement and nervousness, and carrying a little black ring box.

My breath catches.

I watch with an open mouth as he gets down on one knee and opens the box to reveal a softly swirling silver ring with a gorgeous central sapphire stone, off-set by diamonds.

I gasp. "Oh my god."

"Do you like it?"

I nod earnestly. "It's beautiful." My heart pinches and I swallow past a lump in my throat. "It's perfect, Jack. But when did you—"

"Months ago," he says, smiling, but his voice is trembling underneath. It makes me realize the weight of what we're doing. I don't care. I want it. "I knew it was way too soon, but I saw it in the window and couldn't help myself."

He's had this ring for months? He takes my hand in his. "Okay, hush now so I can propose properly."

I grin. "Okay." But I can't resist slipping down and tucking myself into his arms.

"Sam," he says laughing. "You're supposed to stand there."

"Uh-uh." I shake my head. "You have to do it like this."

He laughs again, then his eyes get that tender fire in them and he takes my face in his hands. We're kneeling together on the floor, stomachs and thighs touching, breath mingling. "God, I love you," he says.

"I loved you first."

It's our new joke. He says he was first, because he fell in love with me when I almost died in the hospital, but I didn't fall in love with him until later and he has my drunken escapade to prove it. But I say I win, because even though I thought it didn't count when we weren't having sex, I gave my heart to this boy years and years ago.

But Jack doesn't play the game right now. He's still looking at me with that fire, and holding me so close. "Samantha Lawson," he says, in that way I love, "I promise to do my best to make you happy every day."

<u>You already make me happy every day,</u> I think, but I don't interrupt so he can propose properly.

"You're my favorite girl," he says. "My best girl. You always have been. Will you please be my one and only girl, for the rest of our lives?"

"Yes, Jack," I say, only able to whisper past the lump in my throat. There's nothing I want more.

We're gathered on the second floor patio of Giovanni & Co, a classy restaurant and event hall in Swan Pointe, with a nice view of the ocean. The covered balcony we've reserved looks as it always does, the dark wood-beamed ceiling strung with twinkle lights and little iron lanterns. It has a great atmosphere, so there wasn't anything more we needed to do to it. On one side of the room are two long tables full of food so good, even our resident foodie Chloe has been impressed. There's a small, private bar area in one corner with an ample supply of drinks, and there are high cocktail tables scattered about so people can have a place to set their drinks and food while they talk. There are lovely gas stone fireplaces at the two outer corners of the patio, which keep the space cozy in spite of it being a mild, mid-December evening.

We reserved the room a couple weeks ago and sent out emails and texts, telling people to come in cocktail party dress, prepared for an important announcement.

We've gathered the Firework Girls and their guys, and flew in Jack's family and my mother. We invited a few other key extended family members (including Isabella's mother, who's always kind of mothered me, and who honored me by taking the trouble to come), and friends (mostly Jack's, because that boy knows everybody) who we knew would give the place a festive atmosphere. But aside from making sure the Firework Girls and our parents would be free, we let the chips fall where they may for everyone else, no offense to them.

It's been a good turn-out, though, and now that everyone's had their fill of food and are chatting happily with one another, Jack and I look at one another and smile.

He's wearing a black suit and black tie, but he hates ties, so I loosened the knot when we first got here, and gave him a kiss and said, "Now you look like my Jack."

I'm wearing a form-fitting, sleeveless, silver dress, that's covered in beads, falls to my ankles, and has a delicate slit in the back that goes to my knees. I've worn it several times to Ashley's recitals, and Jack requested it, saying it's his favorite.

Holding my eyes now, and holding my hand, he asks, "Ready?"

"Yes, please."

We each take a deep breath and head over to the front of the balcony. The room slowly falls to an eager silence as people notice what we're doing. They've been pestering us all night about the promised announcement, but we've stayed mum.

All Jack has to do is clear his throat and the last bits of chatter fall away. Still holding hands, we look at one another, grinning.

"Okay," he says. "We have an announcement."

"Really?" Ashley says, smiling. "We had no idea."

Light laughter ripples around the room and I scrunch my face up at her. She does it back.

Jack and I look at one another one last time. Here we go. He faces the gathering and says, "We've set a date to get married."

"I knew it!" Chloe says, beaming.

There are little swells of excitement as people react to Jack's words, but he raises his hand to keep them contained so he can tell them the actual date. After he says it, I watch everyone's faces: confusion, surprise, disbelief. More confusion.

Yeah, this was an awesome idea, I think, grinning.

"But…" Isabella says. "That's today's date."

"Boy, you can't get anything past a Harvard grad," I say, winking at her.

Then the noise on the balcony swells as everyone realizes what's happening.

"Wait a minute," Chloe says, still in shock. "Are you getting married <u>right now?</u>"

Chloe's been knee-deep in wedding plans for several months and still has a few more months to go. We were a little worried she'd be upset at us for cutting in line, but hope she'll understand. I've never been one to fantasize about wedding cakes and bridal bouquets so there wasn't much to plan, and once we made the decision, neither one of us wanted to wait.

We nod at her and I ask, "Is that all right?"

Her face is still puzzling something out. "Hang on. Your invitation was a <u>text.</u>"

"Well, it got you here didn't it?" I shrug and the other girls start to laugh. In another second, Chloe joins in.

She looks at Grayson in amusement. "I'm thinking they may have had the right idea." I'm relieved she's not bothered.

"You just didn't want to be the last Firework Girl to get married, did you?" she asks teasingly.

I wink at her. "We saved the best for last, sweetie."

I turn to Jack, who pulls me to his side while gesturing to one of his clients, Marcus. He's a professional chef and an amateur photographer, he restores classic cars and keeps bees in his backyard, he has two full tat sleeves and a long beard, and is an ordained mail-order minister. We had him over for beer and brats the other day as a thank you for his upcoming service to us, and spent the evening laughing at his decidedly un-minister-like stories. He's the perfect person to marry us.

Marcus works his way to the front, wearing a friendly smile. Jack introduces him to the crowd, then lets him take over. As Marcus brings forward the witnesses who will sign the marriage license later, Jack and I keep looking at each other and smiling.

We're holding each other's hand, and standing so close our arms touch and intertwine, shoulder to inner wrist.

And that's exactly how we stand, looking into each other's eyes, as Marcus begins the simple ceremony we wanted. It's how we stand as we say our vows, and it's how we're standing when we officially become husband and wife.

Still holding my hand, Jack puts his other hand around my waist, and just in time, because I could use his support. He brings his lips to mine and carries me away in that delicious, raging flood that is all Jack.

EPILOGUE

Sam

Chloe's wedding ceremony was one for the books, and the reception we're enjoying is so grand and beautiful, it nearly tops Isabella's.

Chloe's wearing a gorgeous gown with a delicate, applique bodice and a flounced, layered Organza skirt. Her auburn hair is in a graceful updo, with little wisps framing her glowing face. Grayson is the proud and handsome groom, who cannot stop smiling at his new bride.

We're all at the bridal table, sitting through a stream of toasts that are sometimes heartfelt and touching, other times awkward and overly-long, but Chloe and Grayson seem to like each one, so I figure that's what counts. And yes, I toasted them too.

What I didn't do was drink to them.

I didn't drink to any toast.

I just sort of went through the motions, which I figured would be good enough since I'm not exactly the center of everyone's attention right now anyway.

But after the toasts are over and we're back to chatting happily at the table—Chloe on my left and Jack on my right—Isabella calls me out on it. I don't think she means to. She just sort of looks at my still-full glass and absently says, "Hey, Sam, why aren't you drinking your champagne?"

Then she gets this look and her eyebrows shoot up. "Wait, are you pregnant?!"

Suddenly everyone at the table is looking at us.

We didn't want to steal Chloe's thunder. God knows that girl deserves her moment at last, but one look at Jack and I know he's giving it away. He's wearing that big, goofy grin he's been wearing ever since he found out. I can't help it. I smile too.

Chloe squeals and launches herself at me. "Oh, I'm so happy for you!"

From around the table, we're bombarded with exclamations and congratulations and questions about when did we find out and how am I feeling and when am I due.

It's a little overwhelming, but Jack and I keep exchanging grins anyway.

"You're going to be <u>such</u> a great mom," Ashley says.

I give her a grateful smile. I'm not at all sure I'll be a good mom, but I'm determined not to let that get the better of me. I'll try my best.

"I don't know about that. But Jack will be a great dad."

I have <u>no</u> doubts there.

"Oh my gosh," Isabella says, "I can just see it. Jack's going to be the fun dad who makes his kids feel awesome and loved, even when he has to use his dad voice." I glance at Jack; he's blushing. Actually <u>blushing.</u> So freaking adorable.

"And Sam, you're going to be like those cool Italian moms. You're going to have that strong, steady love that your kids can count on, and a kitchen that constantly overflows with food." My eyes are wide on Isabella, drinking in her every word. Will that be me? "And anyone who tries to mess with your kid will regret it for the rest of time."

"Well, that's for damned sure!" I say, and everyone laughs.

"Yet she can be so <u>tender</u> and <u>nurturing</u> when she wants to be," Jack says, teasing me and rubbing my shoulders.

"Cut it out," I say sternly, and everyone laughs again. "I just hope I make it through the newborn stage without breaking it."

"You'll be fine," Ashley says.

"But they're so bitty."

Ashley shrugs. "They're tougher than you'd think."

"Just like you," Jack says, throwing his arm around my shoulder and giving me the kind of look that makes me pay attention. "Bitty but tough."

I lean over and give him a kiss. God, I love this man. "This poor kid will have to be tough, with parents like us."

"She'll have the coolest parents ever." Jack leans back easily.

"She?" Chloe asks excitedly. "Is it a girl?"

"We don't know yet."

"It's a girl," Jack says confidently. I don't know why he feels so sure. I haven't admitted I think it's a girl, too.

Isabella raises her glass, smiling broadly. "A toast! To the next Firework Girl."

I smile as we all raise our glasses. We clink our glasses and drink (except me of course), and the table eventually dissolves into the happy chatter that marks so much of our time together.

I think back to when it all started. Back then, it was just Isabella, Chloe, Ashley and me, sitting around Delsa's diner, downing obscenely huge plates of Volcano fries.

Now here we are, each of us married and me with a baby on the way.

How things change.

But I know one thing with certainty. No matter what comes our way, no matter what changes the future brings, the Firework Girls are forever.

The End

Author's Note

I was tempted to give Sam a nice, tidy ending with her father. I was tempted to give you, the reader, reassurance that he won't be hanging over her head any more. After all as romance readers, we're fans of the Happily Ever After. However, I felt that would be an injustice to the many, many people who have to live their entire lives with a toxic parent, with no easy out and no tidy ending. Sam's power is this: regardless of what her father does or does not do, she found it within herself to create her own happy ending.

Perhaps someone reading this is an adult child of an alcoholic like me (mine is of the "functioning alcoholic" variety, thankfully), or carries unwanted programming due to growing up in a stressful environment that felt out-of-control (like being raised by strict authoritarian parents, neglectful parents, chronically ill parents, codependent parents, or parents who are addicts of any sort). If so, education about the way these childhood environments can affect us as adults is critical, and a good support person or two to help with the sometimes frightening experience of deprogramming is invaluable.

Sam's story touched me in ways I didn't plan.

To all the Sam's out there, Be the Dragonfly. Yo.

About the Author

Jordyn White writes steamy romances featuring smart, sexy women and the swoon-worthy men who adore them. Her sexy love stories are full of passion but don't skimp on the tenderness. She's addicted to trendy coffee houses, poolside lounging, and HEAs. When not tapping blissfully away on her laptop, she takes time to enjoy life with her husband and their children.

JordynWhiteBooks.com

Lightning Source UK Ltd.
Milton Keynes UK
UKHW010647260722
406393UK00003B/637